RACHEL SINCLAIR
THE TRIAL

BOOKS

By Rachel Sinclair

Southern California Legal Thrillers

Presumed Guilty
Justice Delayed
Insanity Defense
Wrongful Conviction
The Trial

Vinci Books

vinci-books.com

Published by Vinci Books Ltd in 2025

Copyright © Rachel Sinclair 2019

The author has asserted their moral right to be identified as the author of this work in accordance with the Copyright, Designs and Patents Act 1988. This work is a work of fiction. Names, characters, places and incidents are the product of the author's imagination or are used fictitiously. Any resemblance to actual persons, living or dead, places and incidents is entirely coincidental.

All rights reserved. No part of this publication may be copied, reproduced, distributed, stored in any retrieval system, or transmitted in any form or by any means, including photocopying, recording, or other electronic or mechanical methods, nor used as a source for any form of machine learning including AI datasets, without the prior written permission of the publisher.

The publisher and the author have made every effort to obtain permissions for any third party material used in this book and to comply with copyright law. Any queries in this respect should be brought to the attention of the publisher and any omissions will be corrected in future editions.

A CIP catalogue record for this book is available from the British Library.

Paperback ISBN: 9781036702946

The EU GPSR authorised representative is Logos Europe, 9 rue Nicolas Poussion, 17000 La Rochelle, France
contact@logoseurope.eu

Printed and bound in Great Britain by Clays Ltd, Elcograf S.p.A.

Chapter One

LORINDA

October 15

LORINDA JAMISON DID the Chinese splits on stage right in front of a well-dressed guy with dark hair, blue eyes, and a big smile. He had been drinking at the strip bar where she worked, since 9 o'clock in the morning, and it was now probably around 2 or so. Lorinda had no idea what time it was, as this bar, like most bars like it, had no clocks. It was also always dark inside, so, no matter what time of the day it was, it always felt like midnight to Lorinda.

Then again, her life always felt like midnight.

She lay down on her stomach, with her legs splayed out behind her, and the good-looking guy, who now was completely schnockered, playfully put a $20 bill into her bustier. He looked right at her and licked his lips.

Lorinda took a deep breath, feeling the sense of burnout that she had been feeling for quite a while. It wasn't necessarily that she hated what she was doing. On the contrary, being an exotic dancer was actually a job that gave her a sense of satisfaction. She had to keep her body in shape, otherwise there was no way in hell she could do the acrobatics on the pole she was able to perform – her legs, which were strong enough to crack a walnut, would be clutching the stripper pole, while the rest of her body hung down, a movement much harder than it looked. Well, maybe – because she knew it looked damned difficult. All those middle-aged housewives who took pole dancing a few years back had no idea what they were in for. That was probably why that particular exercise fad faded away so quickly, because hardly anybody could do what she and the other dancers could do.

It wasn't just the fact that she took a special pride in her body and what it could do on stage, but also the fact that she felt powerful over the men who would come to see her, that gave her such satisfaction. It was a special sense of giving them what they wanted, but only up to a point, teasing them, making them think she was into them, so they would give her $20 tips instead of $10 ones. In reality, not one of those guys would ever have a chance with her, no matter what he looked like, and no matter what he did. She was a one-man woman, and that man's name was Frankie. Well, she wasn't really a one-man woman, so much as she was a one-boy woman – Frankie, at the age of seven, certainly could not qualify as being a man.

But, then again, Frankie was more mature than any of the guys she met at this club.

Frankie was why she was feeling a sense of burnout. She wanted to be with him a lot more than she was. Most of the time, because she had been working at this club for so long, she could choose her hours, and she would choose the hours Frankie was in school. He went to elementary school at 8:30 in the morning and would be home around 3:30 every afternoon. So she chose to work those particular hours. She knew she would still get quite a lot of business even during the day, because that was how it usually was. There were quite a few men who would come in during the lunch hour, for a little escapist fantasy in the middle of the day, along with probably quite a few men who'd told their wives they were at the office but were really spending the day stuffing her bra and G-String with $20 bills. So, even though she did not work at night, she still made some good money while Frankie was in school.

That all worked out very well until recently.

Now, Frankie was not in school. He was at home and she wanted to be with him.

The handsome guy with the dark hair was still staring at her, his perfect teeth gleaming in the glow of the bar. He winked at her and took another drink. "How would you like to go with me into a private room?" he asked her, slurring his words. "I could very much make it worth your while."

She didn't necessarily want to do that, because she knew what men expected when they went to the private room. Not that they were entitled to it. But they seemed to have the attitude that if they were going to pay her the rate the club charged for these private rooms, they expected to get something in return. But she'd been working at the club for long enough to know that she did not have to do what she didn't want to.

And this club had a very strict "no touch" policy - the men were never to touch the dancers, except to put money in their g-strings and bras. Still, the men always expected to be able to not just touch the dancers, but get sexual favors as well. That was why Lorinda hated going back into the private rooms.

When she first started working there, she had to go into

these private rooms when they asked her. She had no choice in the matter. But now, she could say no, and her boss would not be upset with her.

She thought about Frankie, about what he needed. That was literally the only thing she ever thought about anymore. She knew that with his illness, she needed to make as much money as possible. The hospital bills were starting to really mount up and she was having an argument with the insurance company as it was. She could not afford a decent insurance policy for Frankie and she made slightly more than the threshold to be eligible for the Child Health Insurance Program, commonly known as CHIP, which was available to people who made $31,000 or under a year. So she had to go to the free market to get her insurance payment plan for him, while she did not have insurance at all. The most she could afford was a plan with a $15,000 deductible and co-pays for everything. She never imagined she would be blowing through that deductible so quickly, but then again, she never imagined she would have a child who would come down with a very rare form of cancer. Mesothelioma, which was caused by exposure to asbestos, was rare in adults, and exceedingly rare in children of Frankie's age.

In fact, his cancer was so rare that the doctors wanted to treat him with experimental drugs, because, as of now, there wasn't much of a treatment protocol for what he had. At least, there was not yet a treatment protocol for young children with the disease. Even Frankie's subtype of mesothelioma was rarer than rare - he had the disease in the lining of his heart, and this particular type of cancer had affected so few children that there was very little research done on it, so her doctors were shooting in the dark.

It didn't help that she could not afford to see a specialist,

The Trial

because the one specialist who knew something about Frankie's kind of cancer was located at the Mayo Clinic in Minnesota. Traveling to Minnesota was a nonstarter for Lorinda, especially because her insurance company wouldn't pay for it. She could barely get them to pay for treatments he was going through right here in San Diego. If they would've paid for the specialist, she would've definitely tried to make some sacrifices to make it work. She would've done anything to help her son. But her insurance company had made it clear they were not going to pay for the specialist, so she had to make do with the doctors right there in San Diego, the doctors who had never seen a case of a child Frankie's age with the type of cancer he had, so they had no idea what they were doing when they were treating him.

So, she worked. She did whatever she had to do to get the money together to pay for her living expenses, and Frankie's. She took in a roommate, Sherry, who worked the night shift, from 8 PM to 3:30 in the morning, and she had a kid too, so the agreement was that Lorinda would watch Sherry's kid when Sherry went to work, in exchange for Sherry watching Frankie during the hours that Lorinda was in the bar working. Because Frankie was home most days, instead of being in school, because he just did not have the energy to get out of bed, Lorinda needed somebody to care for him while she was at work. And it worked out, because the two roommates were able to split the rent on a three-bedroom apartment, which was everything to her, as San Diego was not known to be a reasonably- priced city as far as rent goes. So Lorinda thought it was two birds one stone, in that she had a sitter for her kid and somebody to split expenses with her.

She reluctantly went to the private room with the dark-haired guy, who told her his name was Robert, but she had a feeling that was just a name he was giving her. A name he pulled out of a hat.

She noticed his left hand was sporting a very conspicuous tan line around his ring finger. She had to have a chuckle about that, because who did he think he was fooling? And who cares? The answer to that was nobody, but she could not afford to call him on his bullshit. Literally. She decided to do what she had to do - get through it and hopefully earn the hundred dollar or more tip she would get from being back there with him.

About an hour later, she emerged from the private room, $500 richer, and trying to forget what she let him do in that room. She closed her eyes and saw her only motivation for doing any of this.

Her boss, Michelangelo, found her and told her it was time for her to go home. "Your shift has been over for the past half hour, so it's time for you to clock out."

She breathed a sigh of relief and then went back into the dressing room, and put on her regular clothes – jeans, T-shirt, and a battered pair of Converse running shoes, a relic from the days when she was a marathon runner. Sometimes she thought about those days, when she was a university student at the University of California San Diego, with the hopes of studying marine biology. That was before she found out she was pregnant with Frankie and had to drop out. She danced while at the University, so she dropped her classes in favor of the easy money she made at the club. She even danced when she was nine months pregnant, because she found there were quite a few men who had a fetish about seeing a pregnant woman with minimal clothing. Then, even after he was born, she was back to work within weeks, because she literally could not afford to do anything else.

The Trial

When she started dancing, she never imagined it would be a long-term thing, but here she was, 8 years later, and she was still dancing.

She stepped out into the bright sunlight, which was always a shocking thing after having been in the bar for so many hours, and it always took her a few minutes to adjust to the light. Then she made her way to the bus stop, which was right across the street from her club, and waited for the first of two buses that would take her to her apartment in the neighborhood of Ocean Beach. She knew she was paying more for what she had, because she was close to the beach – the apartment she shared with Sherry was less than 1000 square feet, even though it was a three bedroom, which meant that every bedroom was tiny, as was the living room and the tiny galley kitchen. No dining room, so everybody ate on TV trays.

She knew she could get a much nicer place for what they were paying for their tiny apartment, which was $3500 a month, if she would be willing to live more inland. Maybe El Cajon or Lakeside or another suburb in East County. But she chose to live by the beach because Frankie loved the water. He always did, even when he was a tiny toddler. She would take him to the ocean and could not get him out of the water. His chubby legs would stomp with delight in the surf, and his tiny hands would clap together while he giggled and sat down in the sand. She had never seen so much joy in any one person as she saw in her son when he was in the water. Such joy was infectious to her, and made her laugh and smile, and uplifted her own spirits. So she decided she was never going to live very far away from the ocean, even if she had to pay a premium for the luxury.

This was more important than ever to her. She herself could take the beach or leave it. She didn't like the heat, the crowds, the sand getting into every crevice of her body. She always had to slather on a ton of sunscreen, for she was exceedingly fair, unlike Frankie, who apparently got his father's genes, as his father was a dark-eyed, dark-skinned Italian man who date-raped her on the only night she had agreed to go out with him. He never knew he had a son and he never would know that. There was no way that she would ever, ever, let Frankie know how he was conceived.

She knew it would be easier if she would have simply let Salvatore know that he had a son, and she could have demanded child support from him, probably a lot of child support from him, considering he was an heir to a fortune and was living off a massive trust fund. But she knew that any child support from him would mean he would have partial custody of him as well – he would deny he raped her, of course, and it would be "he said she said," so he probably would get at least 50% custody if he had to pay child support. She wasn't going to do that. Plus, she couldn't risk Frankie being around Salvatore's extended family - any family who would raise a rapist was not a family she wanted her child to be exposed to. For that matter, she would never want her child to be exposed to a rapist, period. And that's what Salvatore was – a rapist.

So she had to get along as a completely single mother, with no means of support except for herself. She had no real education to speak of, as she had to drop out of college when she was only a freshman. For now, dancing was her life, and she had to scrimp and save every penny, because she knew there was going to come a time she would age out of her chosen profession. She had no plan B, so she was going to have to have some kind of retirement fund to live off of. Now, with Frankie sick, and the doctor bills piling up, there really wasn't much that went

The Trial

into her retirement account, such as it was. No matter how many Roberts were willing to pay her $500 for an hour of private teasing in an isolated room, she could not get ahead.

She got home and immediately saw Sherry was laying on the couch, with her son, Eric, who was the same age as Frankie. Frankie was nowhere to be seen and Lorinda knew what that meant.

She went into the bedroom Frankie shared with Eric. The two boys had bunk beds, Frankie on bottom, Eric on top, Frankie with *Star Wars* bed sheets, Eric with *Avengers*, which was the opposite of their backpacks, as Eric had a *Star Wars* backpack, while Frankie had an *Avengers* backpack.

She sat down on the bed and put her hand on Frankie's forehead. He was fast asleep, and she knew that if she asked Sherry, she probably would tell her that he'd been sleeping all day. That was all he seemed to do anymore.

Oh, he had some good days, where he actually had the energy to go out to the beach, and stand in the water, although his legs never stomped in the water the way they did when he was a tiny baby, for that sense of joy and wonder had long since left him. Yet, on those rare early evenings when Frankie made it out to the beach, he managed a smile. Lorinda had no idea if the smiles that he plastered on his face when she took him out to the water were genuine smiles, or if he simply made happy facial expressions because he wanted to make her happy. She might never know the answer to that question, but she did know that Frankie was the kind of boy who would do anything to please her. And he knew, he had to have known, that his deteriorating medical condition was bringing her to the depths of despair. She tried to hide it, much like he tried to hide his pain and sadness from her. She was pretty good at faking smiles for him, which was why she strongly suspected his smiles were fake as well.

Sometimes she wanted to talk to him about his illness. She wanted him to not be afraid of what was probably going to happen to him. She wanted him to not fear death. Yet, she could never bring herself to have *that* talk with him. Every time she went into his room, with the determination that she was going to have that heart-to-heart, the lump in her throat caught so that she couldn't get any words out, and the two of them never did talk about the impending end of his young life.

He knew he was dying. Children always knew. He knew that most of the kids he'd met in the oncology ward during his hospital stays were, by and large, no longer around. Sometimes she thought that maybe he wanted to talk to her about what he was feeling, but he was a sensitive boy, and he knew that if he was frank with her and told her he knew he would die soon, she would break down. And he wasn't wrong. She *would* break down. She knew that, so the upshot was that neither she nor he ever had the talk about what was going to happen.

Looking at him as he lay in his bed, so tiny and breathing so hard, as the cancer had put him into heart failure, she was afraid he was going to measure his life in hours, not days or weeks as she had hoped. With every breath he took, it seemed like she held her own. His chest would rise, and rise, and rise again, before it fell. She had seen this pattern with her mother, right before her mother's own heart exploded in her chest.

She took a hold of his wrist and felt his pulse, which was thready and light, which seemed to contradict the enormous breaths he was taking in his sleep. She wondered if she should take him back to the ER, but she knew that if she

The Trial

took him to the ER every time she was concerned about his breathing pattern in his sleep that he would spend his entire life in the ER.

She finally tore herself away from Frankie's bed, and went into the living room, and sat next to Sherry and Eric. She took a deep breath, and willed back the tears.

"He's been asleep for most of the day," Sherry said to Lorinda. "I've been checking on him every half hour."

Lorinda looked at her hands, which were clasped so tightly together that her knuckles were white. "We're going to go through another round of chemo, which starts next week. I just hope that –"

She didn't want to say the next words. She didn't want to say out loud what she was thinking. For what she was thinking was that she hoped Frankie could live long enough to take his next round of chemo. That was what she always hoped for - just live long enough to get to his next treatment. None of it did much good, because his cancer was just so rare that nobody really knew how to treat it.

Sherry nodded. She knew the words that were unsaid. She knew.

"So, what are you guys watching?" Lorinda asked Sherry.

Sherry just shrugged. "I don't know, something on Netflix. Eric wanted to watch it."

At that, Eric gave Lorinda a dirty look, which told Lorinda that he was trying to watch the movie, whatever it was, and did not appreciate her talking. She decided to not say anything more, but to take a little walk to her favorite coffee shop, which was just down the street. She would be back before eight, which was when Sherry went to her own shift at the bar. Then she would watch both Eric and

Frankie while Sherry danced at the club until the wee hours of the morning.

The coffee shop she loved was called the OB Garden Cafe. It was a cute little place that was vegan/vegetarian, with high wood ceilings, hardwood floors, and an open-air patio that was dog friendly. She always tried to make the rooftop yoga on Sundays at four, whenever she wasn't working on Sundays, and she really liked to frequent this place because there often were dogs out on the patio that she could pet, and, since she could not have a dog of her own in her small apartment, she got her dog fix there by petting other people's pooches.

Before she sat down, she noticed a familiar face across the room. Regina Baldwin was a friend of her's from way back when. Regina used to work at the same club she worked at, also as an exotic dancer. But the last she heard, Regina left the dancing scene to strike out on her own as a private detective.

After Regina left the club, Lorinda didn't really talk to her that much, as what happens when people leave their place of employment. That always made her sad – you really get to know somebody, you really start feeling comfortable with sharing your innermost thoughts and secrets, then that person leaves, and, at first, you try to keep in touch, calling each other every few weeks, and having lunch once in a while. Then the calls get less frequent, you start making excuses not to have lunch, and so does the other person – you're both so busy that it's very hard to make time in your schedule – and then one day, you realize you haven't talked to the other person in quite a while.

At first, Lorinda tried to pretend she didn't see Regina. She just thought it would be an uncomfortable conversation, because, truth be told, she felt that she was more responsible for the friendship dropping than Regina was. She felt inferior that Regina was making something of herself while she, herself, stayed on at the bar, still dancing for money. She felt left behind. Every time Regina would tell her about all the exciting cases she was working, Lorinda felt a little stab of jealousy go through her heart. She knew in her gut, in her soul, that what she was doing at the moment was all that she would ever be doing. She didn't have the same kind of intelligence and talent Regina and some of the other girls who managed to make it out of the exotic dancing scene had. She didn't have the instincts or investigation skills that Regina had acquired, and she didn't have the kind of guts it took to be a private investigator. And she knew that Regina had another ace in the hole, that helped her get out of dancing for good – her friend, Avery Collins, a lawyer who was Regina's cellmate in prison. Avery took a chance on Regina and helped her break into the PI business.

Lorinda didn't have anybody to help her break into anything, so she really saw no way out of her dancing career. Regina made it out, so Lorinda didn't want to associate with her anymore. Regina just made her feel bad.

Unfortunately, or fortunately, depending on how you looked at it, Regina did notice Lorinda at the coffee shop. As Lorinda sat down, Regina came over to her table, and sat down as well.

"Hey, you, where you been hiding? You know, I've been trying to call you for quite a while, and you never answer your phone. Maybe I should take the hint, but I'm not one to take hints like that. So, how the hell are you?" Regina asked as she leaned forward at the table.

Lorinda just shrugged. She was on the verge of bursting out crying. That was the reason why she came to the coffeehouse, because she didn't want to start bawling in front of her roommate, let alone her own son. A simple question like asking how she was doing just brought everything up.

"Oh, so I guess you're not talking to me," Regina said. "I see how you are. Of course, I didn't think that you of all people would shut me down like this, but I guess it's true that you really never know somebody. Have a nice life."

Lorinda, to her own surprise, started to rapidly shake her head as Regina pushed away from the table. "No, I'm happy to see you. It's just that –" and then she started to shake her head again. "I, I'm going through something right now."

Regina sat back down, as if she suddenly realized she misread the situation completely.

She reached her hand over to Lorinda's hand, and covered it. "I'm sorry. I guess I can be a real bitch sometimes. So, what's going on?"

Lorinda shook her head but then she told Regina the story of her son. "Frankie, you remember him, don't you?"

"Of course, your kid. Good kid. Why, what's going on with him?"

Lorinda took a deep breath. "He's sick. He's very sick. He has this kind of cancer, it's very rare in adults. And with kids, there's only been like 100 kids who have ever had this particular kind of cancer. It's mesothelioma, and –"

Regina narrowed her eyes. "Mesothelioma? That's caused by asbestos. By being exposed to asbestos for years and years."

Regina was now very interested in what Lorinda had to say.

Lorinda just nodded. "That's what the doctor says. But I don't know where he would've been exposed to asbestos, and I really don't know how he could have been exposed to as much as he needed to be exposed to in order to get it like this at his age. He's only seven years old. I really don't know how much longer he has. He's my entire life. I mean, my whole life. Everything I do, it's for him. Everything. I don't know how I'm going to have a reason for living after he goes. So, I guess I have to apologize to you for not reaching out more often. Truth be told, I really think I want to join him after he dies."

"Wait. There has to be something you can do for him."

"He's been doing chemo and radiation. I can't afford to get him into some of the experimental treatments that are not offering clinical trials. I've done the research. I know what's out there. I can't get my insurance company to pay for hardly anything. I mean, they pay for chemotherapy and radiation, things like that, but nothing's working for him, and I really want to get him into some of the other treatment options that I found. But I can't. So —"

"Okay. Here's the thing," Regina interrupted. "You have no idea how Frankie got sick, right?"

Lorinda nodded her head. "I mean, he must've been exposed to asbestos somehow."

"You ever use talcum powder on the kid?"

"Actually, no. I've known for a long time that talcum powder is bad. I've heard that for years. I don't use it, and I've never used it on Frankie."

"Have you talked to your landlord? Maybe your apartment has asbestos."

"Yes, that's the first thing I did. And inspectors said they could find no asbestos in my apartment or in my apartment building. I have a readout. I don't understand all of it, but the bottom line is that apparently my apartment and apartment building is clear of asbestos. I also reported my kid's disease to his school, and they opened up an investigation as well, and his school does not have any asbestos either. I suppose it's entirely possible that they're lying, or somebody's lying, I don't know. I just know that I don't have the emotional energy to fight these people. Especially because I don't really know where he got exposed to asbestos. All I know is that he has been."

"Well, we have to figure that out. If we can figure out what happened, how Frankie was exposed, I'm sure we can probably help your doctor in treating him. What kind of experimental therapies are out there now?"

"Immunotherapy. I guess that doctors can use a person's immunity system to fight the cancer. Also gene therapy. I don't really understand too much about that, except for I guess that the person's DNA gets mutated, so doctors can inject new DNA into cells. And there's another one, I don't really understand that one at all. I guess it's kinda like the gene therapy, but just a little bit different. I don't really know, because my insurance company won't cover any of it. So I just have to go with what they know about, and it's killing him. It's literally killing him, faster than the cancer is. Sometimes I think I should just stop. I mean, I don't want to put him through futile torment. I don't want his last days on earth to be miserable."

"Listen, I know you probably don't want to hear this, but you need to fight," Regina said. "Especially because you told me your kid is your life. I'm working for an attorney, Avery, she usually takes criminal cases, but she's a very good trial attorney. Why don't you let her talk to you? I mean, here's the thing. Number one, you need somebody to fight for you against your insurance company. It's bullshit that they're denying your right to try everything you can to get him well. I don't know a whole lot about the experimental therapies they're using for this particular disease, but I do

The Trial

know one thing. Any insurance company that will pay for just radiation and chemotherapy, and not even allow you to try something promising, that's just bullshit. I mean, just because you aren't wealthy, that means that you can't try gene therapy, or immunotherapy, or something like that? I'm going to have to have Avery take a look at your insurance policy and have her try to get the insurance company to get your kid covered. Believe me, insurance companies want you to give up. They want you just to not argue with them when they say they're not going to cover this or that. If you just go along with it, they win. And here you are, paying out the nose to them, and they're just going to not let you try everything you can?"

"I don't know what I can do. I mean, they said it's not covered, and that's what they say."

"Trust me on this, you get a lawyer involved with it, and they're suddenly going to play ball. I've seen that time and time again. But I think you also need to hire a lawyer because you need to figure out how your kid came in contact with asbestos in the first place. And then you need to sue the pants off of whoever poisoned your kid. You can't just take this lying down. This is your kid. It's your life. I know you don't have a lot of money, and that's fine. Avery will take the case, even if you don't have a dime. She'll take it on contingency. Do you know what that means?"

Lorinda fidgeted while she ate the salad that had just arrived at the table. She did kind of know what contingency meant, but not really. It was something about the lawyer not getting paid unless she wins, or something like that. But she was embarrassed to admit that she didn't really know what that term meant. "Yes, I know what it means."

"Okay, then. Listen, I know Avery has an opening tomorrow at three. Why don't you come to her office and she can set you up? She'll go through everything Frankie has been exposed to, and she'll try to figure out exactly what happened. And then she'll sue the crap out of the company that poisoned your kid."

"I can't do that. I have to work. I work every day from nine until three thirty."

"What are you doing these days?" Regina asked.

"Oh, this and that." Lorinda scratched her cheek, her eyes not meeting Regina's. "So, listen, I have to work, or I don't get paid. And if I don't get paid, Frankie's never going to have what he needs. He's never going to be able to die with any dignity. I really want to get him into hospice, but I can't afford that either. So all I can really do is watch him fade away, day by day, hour by hour, minute by minute. That's all I can do."

"Suit yourself," Regina said with a big sigh. "But I'm telling you, there's money to be made here."

That was the wrong thing to say to Lorinda. "Oh, that's your angle? You want to make more money for your boss? Is that all you really care about? What about my son, lying in bed, day after day, sleep being the only thing he has in his life. Because when he's awake, he's in pain. Every breath hurts him. I get up 5-6 times a night, just so I can check on him. I'm in constant fear that I'm going to wake up one morning and find he's dead. He's only seven years old. Seven years old. He hasn't lived his life at all. I mean, not that life is so great, but maybe it would've been for him. But he'll never know. He'll never know, and maybe that's a blessing. I don't know. What I do know is that he's not for sale. No amount of money will ease his pain. So you might just think of him as a meal ticket, but he's not. He's flesh and blood, he's in constant pain, and he's the center of my world. So you can just shove the money to be made up your ass."

She wasn't quite finished with her salad, but she suddenly had no appetite to eat the rest of it. She couldn't believe that Regina, the girl she thought was her friend, could be so callous.

"Would you just relax?" Regina asked. "Listen, I don't think I need to tell you this, but I'm going to anyway. My boss, Avery, she doesn't need your money. She was in the joint for seven years, even though she shouldn't have been in the joint at all. The prosecutor's office nailed her to the wall for something she wasn't good for. Her public defender threw the case for money. She's a millionaire because of it. And she's not the kind a girl who gives shit less about taking cases for money. In fact, she takes a lot of cases *pro bono*. Do you know what that means? I'll tell you what it means. It means that she can't say 'I don't get paid until you get paid,' because she doesn't get paid at all on those cases. But she's happy to do it if she believes in the case. So, I'm only telling you that there's money to be made for your benefit. Listen, you were just telling me you wanted to get experimental treatment for your son. And you tell me the insurance company won't pay for it. I'm trying to say that you win this case and you suddenly got all kinds of money to pay for whatever you want."

Lorinda couldn't hold back the tears. They were hot and streaming down her face. "Don't you see? Can't you understand? How long will that take to get money out of this company? I mean, we don't even know who to even sue at the moment. How long will it take to to get a case to trial? A year? More? My son doesn't have two weeks left."

Regina nodded. "Listen, I know what you're saying. And you're right. It takes a long time to get a case to trial. Even if the case settles, that still takes a long time, because discovery has to go back and forth between the parties, depositions and all that bullshit. Big companies with hired guns like to drag it out as long as possible, make it as painful as possible. They like to scare away people who don't have a lot of money to try a case against them. So, you're right. The case will drag on and on, even if you have a good ground to stand on. But here's what Avery can do - she can also work on getting your insurance company to pay for these experimental treatments. If the insurance company will pay for those treatments, maybe Frankie can get better. You never know."

Lorinda couldn't understand a word Regina was saying to her. She could hear the words coming out of Regina's mouth, but she had never experienced somebody who would do something like that for her. She always thought of lawyers as being shysters, criminals, ambulance chasers. Like they would go to a funeral and pass out their business cards. She didn't trust Regina, but then she thought to herself, *what do I have to lose?*

"Are you sure your boss will do that?"

"No. I'm not sure. That's why I'm going to have to talk to her and see. I'll tell you that this is the kind of thing she does, if she believes in the case enough. Listen, she's the kind of chick who takes capital murder cases for free. That means death penalty cases. Do you know how much work that is? All I can say is that she's good people. You could do worse than to have her on your case."

"What if we can't figure out how he got the disease? What then?"

Regina put her hand on top of Lorinda's hand, and squeezed it. "Trust me, she'll figure it out. You don't know

The Trial

Avery the way I know Avery. She's like a dog after a bone. All I can say is that there's something you've used with Frankie that exposed him to asbestos, and maybe you're just not thinking about it at the moment. It'll come to you. You'll remember, probably in the middle of the night, when you're drifting off to sleep. At least, that's how things come to me. When I'm not thinking about it, it just pops into my head, whatever it is. It will be like that for you too. So why don't you just make an appointment with Avery and you can discuss everything with her?"

Lorinda thought about her son, how he looked as frail and light as a bird, lying in that bed, and she knew she had to do something to help him. She knew that it was a long shot, a Hail Mary. She knew that most of the people with mesothelioma died of it, that the odds were against him. But, at the moment, there was no hope for him at all. Regina was offering at least a little something. She was going to have to take it.

"Okay," she said as she took a drink of her water. "I'll come and see your boss. When did you say she had an opening?"

"Tomorrow at three. Do you have to work?"

"Yes. I do. I can find someone to cover for me, but not on such short notice."

"I'll ask her. Sometimes she makes house calls. In your case, she'd have to come down to the place where you work. Guess you're still working at the Cheetah Club?"

Lorinda felt ashamed. She hated feeling like she was inferior to Regina, but she did. "Well, at the moment, yes. I mean, I'm fixing to go back to school. Finish my degree, maybe get a job working at Scripps," she said, referring to the Scripps Institute of Oceanography, the marine biology research lab in La Jolla. "You know when I was 18, I was studying marine biology. That's always been what I wanted to do. This job won't be my life, or anything."

Regina smiled. "Listen, you think I judge you? You're talking to a girl who popped her old man, who sold her body for money for many years. I know a girl's gotta do what a girl's gotta do. And there ain't no shame in any of it. Ain't no shame in survival. So maybe I'll try to come down to your club with Avery tomorrow. In the meantime, try not to think too hard about how Frankie might've been exposed to asbestos. If you try to focus on it too much, you'll never figure it out. At any rate, Avery will ask a million questions, and maybe something she'll ask you will trip something. You know, maybe you guys took a camping trip one year, and he played in the rock quarry. And are you sure you never use talcum powder with him?"

Lorinda nodded. "I'm positive of that. I mean, I know there's been all kinds of cases where women have died of ovarian cancer that they got from talcum powder, and that's kind of a new thing. But I'm telling you, I learned about talcum powder being harmful way back when. I knew it when I was a kid. I don't remember where I read about it, it might've even been in the *National Enquirer*, my mom used to buy that all the time, but I read about it. And that was just something I never used. And I never used it on Frankie either."

Regina took a deep breath and blew it out slowly. "Well, whatever. Anyhow, I'll be seeing you tomorrow at three?"

"At three."

Chapter Two

AVERY

"OKAY, so let me get this straight. You broke into a water amusement park, after hours, you went down the waterslide, and you hurt yourself. Is that what you're telling me?"

I couldn't quite believe I agreed to meet with this person. Well, actually Colleen, my new assistant fielding my calls, put her on the roster. I was going to have to have a talk with her after this. I hated to have my time wasted, and this was an open and shut waste of time. It was like the case where I had an inquiry from a girl who was in the intersection when a fire truck was coming through and the fire truck hit her. She heard the fire truck barreling down the street, lights and sirens blazing, and yet she ignored it and proceeded on through the light. She told me she wanted to sue the fire truck because he ran a red light and hit her. That was another case where I just couldn't believe I took the time to talk to her. I really couldn't believe someone ended up taking her case. Not on contingency, of course. Nobody would be dumb enough to take a case like that on contingency.

The girl, Brittany, nodded her head and showed me her broken wrist. "Yes. I went down this enormous slide and I hurt myself. There wasn't any water on it, and nobody told me I was supposed to use these big mats to go down it. You're supposed to be able to slide down the slide with these big mats and there must be a lot of water to help you out. So I went down the slide, it was completely dry, I had no mat, and I tumbled off of it and hurt my wrist at the bottom."

I tried to stifle the urge I had, which was to strangle her. "You trespassed. The reason why there was not any water on this slide at the time you slid down it was because it was after hours and the park was closed. You broke into the place. No, there's not going to be any mat to slide down the slide, and yes, the slide will not have any water on it. I'm sorry, but you assumed the risk when you decided to break into the waterpark after hours and go down a water slide without water or mats. Now you might be able to find an attorney out there who will take your case, if you have the money to pay him or her. There's lots of unethical attorneys out there who would be more than happy to take your money. But that's how you know your case is a sure loser – if no attorney agrees to take it on a contingency fee, which means they don't get paid if you don't get paid, then your case is a dead dog loser. What I'm trying to say is beware anybody who wants to take your case for a fee. Whoever would agree to that is simply in it for the money."

I took out a piece of gum out of my drawer and offered it to Brittany. She was now looking extremely annoyed, like she wanted to jump down my throat. "I'm hurt, and it's not my fault, I want that waterpark to pay."

"It's not your fault?" I asked her incredulously. "I want to remind you that you were trespassing at the time you got

The Trial

hurt. I understand you got a citation for that. There's not a judge in this world who will not dismiss your case immediately. And, for good measure, any judge worth his or her salt will make you pay the legal fees of the park, which will be substantial, trust me on this. You see, here's the thing. If you happen to find an unethical attorney who will take your money and file this case, the other side will have to file a motion to dismiss. And they're going to have to pay their attorney, oh, around $1000 an hour, to prepare this motion to dismiss. They're going to take their sweet time preparing this motion to dismiss, filing it, all of that. They're going to rack up $10,000 in legal fees in a single afternoon. That'll just be the beginning. I wouldn't be surprised if they rack up about $50,000 in legal fees, just to teach you a lesson. And the judge will throw your case out and make you pay that $50,000, because this is a frivolous lawsuit if ever I heard of one. Now, I'm very sorry, but I have to go to a club and meet a new client. She has actual problems, problems that were not of her own making. She has a son who's dying and nobody really knows exactly why. You can go down the street and see if you can find a huckster to take your case. No doubt you can. But I'm not going to touch it with a 10-foot pole. I have more ethics than that."

I was just trying to scare her, as California actually didn't have a "loser pays" statute, therefore Brittany wouldn't have to pay the water park's legal fees. If only California would adopt that, it would be a better thing. It would certainly cut down on bogus cases that clog up the legal system like marshmallows trying to go through a straw.

Brittany rolled her eyes. "Well, I see you're not going to help me. So I'll be on my way."

Don't let the door hit you on the way out. "Good luck."

At that, Brittany left.

"Colleen!" I screamed.

Colleen heard me call for her and she appeared at the door. She was a slight redhead, with a splash of freckles dancing around her rather short button nose. She perpetually had a look on her face of startle, because that's just the way her eyes were – they were wide, with the irises taking up not as much space as most other people's irises do, so the whites of her eyes were dominant. Not that she was an unattractive girl. On the contrary, she was quite pretty. But I had to admit that her perpetual expression of alarm unnerved me just a little bit.

"Yeah, what do you need?" she asked me. She was spooning out some yogurt out of a small container, scooping the concoction with gusto, as if she hadn't eaten in days.

"Nothing. I just want you to screen out people who call a little bit better. I don't like to have my time wasted with frivolous claims."

"You told me you wanted to get more into personal injury," Colleen said defensively. "The girl said she was hurt at a waterpark. I thought it sounded like a good one."

"See, here's the thing. You need to dig a little deeper into what these people actually did. Yes, if she was hurt at a waterpark, and it was during the business hours, then I would agree with you. It probably would be a decent case. But that wasn't what happened here. The girl broke into the waterpark and got hurt. Broke into it. As in, trespassing. As in, committing a crime. I hate to say it, but she doesn't have a leg to stand on."

Colleen pointed at me with her spoon. "I don't think that's true. Listen, I've taken classes for my paralegal degree and I studied case law too. And one of the things I learned was that sometimes kids will jump a fence and get hurt in a

The Trial

neighbor's pool, and that neighbor has to pay. What's the difference between that happening and this?"

I rolled my eyes. "I think you know just enough to be dangerous, but not enough to know what you're talking about. You're talking about the attractive nuisance doctrine, which is when a neighbor has a pool but no fence around it. It's just in their backyard and there's no fence, or maybe the gate is open, or something else. Sometimes a kid can get hurt in the pool, even though the kid's trespassing, and the kid might have grounds for a lawsuit. By the way, California does not have the attractive nuisance doctrine anymore, but that's neither here nor there. In this case, this woman broke into that waterpark. She apparently cut the deadbolt to get into the park. So, apples and oranges."

Colleen's pale face turned red and she looked down at her shoes. "I'm sorry," she mumbled. "But people sue for all kinds of stupid things. What about that woman who poured coffee on herself and got millions of dollars for it? What about that?"

This again. "Here's the thing. People seize on cases like the McDonald's coffee lady, and the general impression is that people are earning millions of dollars for stupid things that are their fault all the time. That's because a media sensationalizes a case and doesn't give the public all the information it needs. In that case, with the McDonald's lady, she had to have skin grafts on her thighs. The coffee was that hot. Yes, she poured it on herself - she put it between her legs while she tried to get the lid off of the coffee cup and the coffee spilled out. It could happen to anybody. That doesn't mean that because she had a little accident that she has to go through skin grafts and third-degree burns. And you have to understand that a jury of her peers listened to all the information, everything that happened to her, and they decided to award her millions of dollars. If the lawsuit was that frivolous, it would have been dismissed before it ever got to a jury, and a jury would not have awarded that kind of money for something purely frivolous. There was obviously a there there."

Colleen nodded her head. "Oh, I didn't know about the skin grafts and all that."

"Most people don't know about that, because the media doesn't go into that. But she suffered third-degree burns on her thighs because the coffee was that hot and McDonald's had hundreds of other people complaining about how hot it was and didn't do anything about it. The jury heard the information about that, the facts, and they awarded punitive damages, which means they were trying to punish McDonald's. That's how egregious it was. So I know most people just read the headlines and don't bother to really look into the facts of the case that's splashed in the media. You aren't alone in that. And you're probably not alone in thinking people are awarded a lot of money all the time for frivolous claims. But there's one thing to bear in mind – a truly frivolous claim, one without any merit, will never make it to a jury. And if by some miracle it does make it to a jury and survives summary judgment and motions to dismiss, no jury will award any money to somebody filing a truly frivolous claim. So the next time you read some media headline talking about how this person got $1 million for a boneheaded move that he was at fault for, read a little deeper. You'll find out there's more to the story. In Brittany's case, however, there's not more to the story. The woman will never win a dime."

Colleen seemed like she was chastised and I felt a little sorry for her. "Okay, I'll try to be a little bit more careful when I schedule your appointments."

The Trial

"Thank you. I appreciate that." At that, I picked up my briefcase. "Well, I have to head out to a club to meet a new client who Regina told me about."

"Okay, I'll hold down the fort, but I promise I won't schedule anybody else in who has a bullshit claim."

I smiled. "Well, even if you do, it's not that big of a deal. Sometimes I get a kick out of crazy people."

At that, I headed out the door, into my car, and drove to the Cheetah Club.

Chapter Three

CHEETAH'S WAS a club in the Claremont area of San Diego. It was a typical strip club. There was a stage in the middle of the enormous floor, with a moat-like pit in between the stage and the tables that surrounded the stage. Red chairs buttressed the Pentagon structure of granite tabletops that surrounded the stage. Just beyond the stage area were leather booths with tiny tables in front of them. The club was dark, so, even though it was 3 o'clock in the afternoon, it felt like it was probably midnight. I wondered if that's how the girls felt in this club, disoriented, like it was always in the middle of the night, even though it was clearly in the middle of the day.

The red seats around the stage were filled with men, most of them drinking a beer or cocktail, and, onstage was a beautiful dark-haired girl. She obviously had thighs that could crack walnuts, as she was flipping around the pole, including hanging upside down from the pole by just her thighs and her high-heeled shoes. She was dressed in pasties and a tiny string bikini thong underwear in bright gold. She

The Trial

bent down, coming over to the men sitting at the tables, and most of them stuffed bills into her panties. She went back over to the pole, whipped around it rapidly, and then did the Chinese splits, both of her legs splayed out on either side of her, while her chest hit the floor.

I was always amazed by how athletic these girls were. How flexible. I felt my own thighs and knees creaking in sympathy as I watched this girl do her Chinese splits, and then when she kicked her legs high up in the air, so high her knee hit her face, right before going into the American splits, her right leg forward, left leg back, her chest resting on her right leg. I could picture this girl being a gymnast in her youth, or involved in some other kind of athletic endeavor that demanded superhuman strength and flexibility.

I couldn't help but think this kind of dancing was an underappreciated art.

I looked around and saw Regina was coming in the door. That was good, because I didn't know who I was looking for. I had no idea what this Lorinda looked like. Regina explained that at the moment, Lorinda was on the floor, getting drinks for people. There were quite a few women walking around, most of them topless and wearing tiny g-strings, just like the girl on stage who was entertaining the men.

"Where's your friend?" I asked Regina, yelling over the sound of the loud thumping music piped into the club. "Is she around?"

"Yeah, she's waiting tables, but she's heading back to the dressing room right now. She's taking a break so she can talk to you. She told me there's a private room that's a little bit quieter in the back of the club and her boss will let her have that room for an hour so she could talk to you and tell you everything about her son. She told me to just go backstage and find her when you get here, so, if you'd like to follow me, we'll go find her."

I followed Regina into the backstage area, where there were girls everywhere changing into costumes. Some of the girls were counting their money, while others were busy putting on makeup in front of huge mirrors.

All around, there was the din of friendly banter between the girls.

"Hey, bitches, look at what I got? A Benjamin. From a rando," one of the girls said, flashing her hundred dollar bill. "I just brought him one drink and he tips me a C-Note, yo."

"Aw, man, you must've gotten that hunchbacked dude," another girl said. "Dude must be loaded 'cause he's always flashing around those bills to every girl. You ain't special, in other words."

"Way to make Chelsea feel like crap, there, Lady Q," another girl said, nudging the second girl.

"Anybody got a tampon? My Aunt Flo just came in early." A blonde girl in a green satin G-String.

"Better early than late, huh, Destiny? Or worse yet, not at all."

While all this was going on, Regina looked around the dressing room and then her eyes landed on a slight blonde in the corner of the room. She had a look of wide-eyed innocence, so she looked much younger than her 26 years. I knew she was 26, because Regina told me she was. But, looking at her, I would've never guessed that. I would have guessed her to be around 18. Her skin was alabaster white, her eyes were big and cornflower blue, and she looked like the kind of girl a guy would be drawn to in a club like this. She probably had quite a few admirers who wanted to

The Trial

protect her, take her home, keep her safe. She probably reminded more than one man of their daughters.

When she looked right at me, I saw something else in her eyes — a look of sadness. A haunted expression, as if she'd seen something terrible in her life, like a war, or maybe seeing a loved one die right before her eyes. She looked at Regina and a small smile played across her face. It was not a happy smile, but a shy one. If I could get a read on her, I would say she was somebody who was beautiful but insecure, maybe somebody who let men take advantage of her, and the reason why she would let them do it is because she didn't feel she could do any better.

Regina led me over to the woman then put her hand on her shoulder. "Avery, this is Lorinda. Lorinda, Avery. She's the one I told you about, the one who's going to get to the bottom of all this and make sure your son has every chance to beat this thing."

I felt uncomfortable when Regina said that. I knew something about mesothelioma. It wasn't curable and the survival rate for five years was only 12%, sometimes less. I hoped Regina wasn't telling this woman that I could help her find a cure for her son, because I didn't think I could. The most that could happen at this point would be if her son could go into remission, maybe even long-term remission, but he would never be completely free of the disease. Unless, of course, he was able to survive for long enough that he could live to see a cure. I knew there were cutting-edge treatments available that were being discovered all the time, and perhaps a cure for the disease was right around the corner.

But, I also knew the odds were stacked against the poor kid. Especially because, according to Regina, the kid was already very sick. It wasn't like he was in the early stages.

That was always a key to long-term survival rates for cancer victims – finding it early. It didn't help that the insurance company was restricting this kid to the usual chemotherapy and radiation treatments, especially because these treatments apparently were not working. If Frankie could have access to some of the more cutting-edge treatments that were available, including immunotherapy, which uses the body's own immunity as therapy; genetic therapy, which uses healthy cells to kill cancer cells; photodynamic therapy, which uses a light-activated drug called a photosynthesizer to kill cancer cells; and anti-angiogenic therapy, which uses drugs to prevent tumors from forming new blood vessels, then he might have had a chance.

Yes, it was true that chemotherapy and radiation were still the most common way of treating the disease, but when it doesn't work, like in this case, you have to try something else. And the fact that her insurance company was denying further treatment was abhorrent to me. I didn't understand why her insurance company was denying everything. That was the first thing I would have to do - review her policy and write some sternly worded letters that would tell them in no uncertain terms that they were going to have to cover different therapies.

Lorinda smiled at me, but it was as if she was a tiny little bird who was gently cocking her head to and fro. She seemed as fragile as a sparrow and there was no joy in her expression. My heart sunk as I realized that any kind of light that was ever behind those eyes was extinguished through a lifetime of pain.

"It's good to meet you," she said, extending one bony hand for me to shake. As with the rest of her body, her hands were extremely pale, except for the nails that were colored a bright blue. I looked at her face, and I could see her swallowing, her neck was that delicate. "Regina tells me you might be able to do something for me, but I'm not going to get my hopes up. I can't ever get my hopes up, because every time I do, something comes along and snatches it all away. And if you met my son, you would understand. There's really not a whole lot of hope there."

"We'll take things one thing at a time. That's always the key to any case. Just take things step-by-step. Now Regina told me there was a private room your boss will let us go into and talk?"

She nodded. "Follow me."

She walked back to a maze of rooms and opened the door to one of them. "This is a room where the girls can entertain a private client. I can turn off the music here." At that, she took out a remote control and killed the music blasting through the speakers in the room. "Go ahead and sit down. And thank you for coming to see me. I would've come to see you, but I can't afford to leave my job for any period of time. I would've had to take a bus, several buses down to your office, and several buses back, so I would've missed the rest of my shift. And I don't get off until 4 o'clock today, because I'm talking to you, so I have to make up that hour. I really don't know exactly what I hope to get out of this meeting. As I was telling Regina, I have no idea how my kid was exposed to asbestos."

I nodded. And then I looked at my notes. I had transcribed everything Regina told me about what Lorinda told her about her kid. "I see you've never used talcum powder with him. I also see you sent crews to test the school where he goes to and your own apartment building, and all of that has come up negative for asbestos. So we're going to have to dig a little deeper to find out where the exposure might've come from. I've done some research online and I discovered other possible avenues we can look at. One is crayons. There are certain brands of crayons that have been recalled from toy stores and dollar stores because they have asbestos in them. Now, here's the thing – it's very difficult to get mesothelioma from eating a crayon. It's highly unusual for the child would get mesothelioma in the first place, because usually mesothelioma comes from repeated exposure from years and years, and it doesn't usually show up for years after the exposure. It's not unheard of - it's very rare, but not impossible, for a child to get mesothelioma from asbestos. But, I'll be honest with you, even if your kid is the kind of kid who eats his crayons, I would be very surprised if he would to get mesothelioma from that. But, at the same time, that's something we have to look at."

Her blue eyes blinked rapidly. "I only buy him Crayolas and I bought them at Walmart. Is that one of the brands of crayons that's been recalled?"

I looked quickly at my phone and saw that Crayola was one of the brands that did *not* test positive for asbestos. Other brands, like Playskool, Disney and brands like that, brands that were not as well-known as Crayola, had toxic levels of asbestos. "You're positive you've only bought him Crayolas? No other brand?"

"No other brand."

I tapped my fingers on the table. "What about the kids at school? Do you think one of them might have had some other brand of crayons and maybe lent him their crayons?"

"I suppose. I don't really know. And even if that happened, how would we even prove it? It's not like a teacher has told me she caught him eating crayons or anything like that."

"Well, that's always the rub. If we know that one of his friends at school had some kind of contaminated crayons, we might be able to make a case to the jury that that was how he got his disease. But I will admit, it's not a solid case. Not as solid as if he himself had a contaminated crayon box you bought him. Even then, we'd have to not only hope you kept the crayons in question, which is always unlikely, because I know parents are always throwing out their kids' crayons after the school year is out, but if you kept it, we would have it tested, and if it tested positive for asbestos, that would be a pretty decent case. But you're right, if it was some other kid's crayon and the teacher didn't catch him in the act of eating this other crayon, it would be very difficult to prove causation. So we're going to have to move on."

Lorinda nodded but said nothing.

"Okay," I continued. "There was another recall I found online, and that was that certain magic kits were being recalled because they contained asbestos. Did you happen to buy Frankie any kind of magic kit, like for Christmas or something like that?"

Lorinda shook her head. "No he was never interested in magic or anything like that. So, no."

I was running out of ideas as to where Frankie could've been exposed to asbestos, at least in the amount he needed to be exposed to in order for him to have gotten this disease at such a young age. "So, no talcum powder, no contaminated crayons, no magic kits, your building and the school has been tested. There is one other thing that could've possibly caused this. And that's cosmetics. Some brands of cosmetics have been recalled because of asbestos. Now I know that he's seven years old and he's a boy, so he probably does not wear face powder and cosmetics like that. But it's entirely possible that maybe your face powder has asbestos in it, and he's been around you when you're putting it on, so he was infected that way. Is that a possibility?"

"I suppose. I wear face powder, but I try to wear face powder that's natural. I buy it through the Internet, and I try to find the most natural brand possible. That's what's so ironic - I've been a stickler for organic products. I don't like a lot of chemicals in my environment, or in my food. I even use cleaning products that are natural. I buy them from Whole Foods."

I took a deep breath. "Well, I guess it's worth a shot. If I could go to your house, and test your face powder, maybe that's where it came from." However, I knew that I would be barking up the wrong tree when it came to the face powder. If Lorinda was telling the truth, and she had no reason to lie, then it would be extremely unlikely that her face powder would've been the culprit. From what I read online, the face powders and cosmetics that had the asbestos in them came from Claire's boutique, and I got the distinct impression they were probably on the cheaper end of things.

My head was starting to hurt. "Well, I just wonder if I could possibly have a look around your apartment sometime. Sometime soon. Maybe I can figure it out if I went over there and looked at everything in your place. I'm not making any promises, but maybe something will spark an idea in my head."

"Of course. I get off work at 4 o'clock today. You can come over to my apartment this evening if you want. You can get a chance to meet Frankie if you come over. I mean, he doesn't do much more than sleep anymore, but he has good days and bad days. Some days I come home and he's sitting up in bed watching television, eating a hamburger from In-N-Out. That's his favorite restaurant, In-N-Out. I mean, I could give him a choice between going to a fancy steakhouse or In-N-Out, and he'll choose In-N-Out every time. Me, I'm more of a Burger Lounge type of gal, although I do like me some Hodad's from time to time." Hodad's was considered to be an Ocean Beach staple. It was a burger place where people lined up outside, literally. I'd never been there, but had always wanted to try it, just because there is something about seeing a line of people outside a restaurant that makes you feel compelled to see what all the fuss is about. FOMO and all that.

As for In-N-Out, I could never see what the fuss was about that one. I'd had better hamburgers at Wendy's. But for the people who loved that restaurant, they were willing to wait any amount of time to get their order. Turned out that the name In-N-Out was a misnomer, because you certainly did not get in and out of the place anytime soon.

"I would like to come to your apartment this evening," I said. "I would like to meet Frankie and I would like to take a look around and see if there's anything that makes me suspicious. And, for sure, I want to review your insurance policy. I have some connections over at Blue Cross/Blue Shield, which is the insurance company I know that you use. I'll see what I can do as far as getting his illness covered by nontraditional treatments."

As I looked at Lorinda, I realized there was perhaps a spark of hope in her eyes when she first saw me. But, in seeing her eyes now, she looked even deader than when I first came in. I realized my meeting with her probably extinguished any ember of hope that she might have had that her son might actually survive.

I was going to have to get her justice, somehow someway.

But first, I was going to have to figure out exactly how Frankie was exposed to asbestos.

Chapter Four

AFTER I MET with Lorinda at the club, I decided to see a friend of mine who was an expert that I'd used in earlier cases. Dr. Ramirez was a distinguished epidemiologist who was usually available to testify as an expert in cases where there are disease clusters that can be explained by environmental causes. I had used him in a case that I took on a few years back, where kids were getting sick from contaminated groundwater. I was able to pinpoint that the contaminated groundwater had come from a chemical company who was improperly disposing of its waste. That was the only class action suit I'd been involved with of that magnitude, as my bread and butter had always been criminal cases. But, in that case, I'd gotten involved because another friend of Regina's had a sick kid and she wanted me to look into it.

I just had a hunch that seeing Dr. Ramirez was going to enlighten me.

I went to his office, which was in a high-rise downtown, and he greeted me with a big smile and warm hug. Dr. Ramirez was around 60 years old, black hair, olive skin, a goatee and perfect white teeth that he displayed often, as he usually had a big smile on his face. I had always liked him, as he was a guy of good humor and great warmth.

"Avery, Avery, come in. Long time no see, huh? To what do I owe this great pleasure?"

"I have a case. It's a very unusual case, and I thought maybe you might give me some ideas about what I can look for when I proceed."

He nodded and motioned to the chair in front of his desk. "I'm all ears. What's on your mind?"

I sat down, crossed my legs, and looked at his desk. "Here's the thing. There's a boy, he is living with his mother, seven years old. He has a very rare type of cancer. It would be rare even in an adult, and it's so rare in children that there's only been less than 100 childhood cases reported over the years. I wanted to ask you what you thought about this case."

" Go ahead, what does this kid have?"

"Mesothelioma. But it's not pleural," which meant it wasn't attacking Frankie's lungs, "and it's not peritoneal," which meant it wasn't attacking Frankie's abdomen. "It's actually pericardial," which meant the cancer affected the sac around Frankie's heart.

Dr. Ramirez looked startled when I told him Frankie had pericardial mesothelioma. "That's a true rarity. And you're right, there have been so few cases of a child with this kind of disease that there haven't been any studies done. But here's the thing. You're right that there've only been less than 100 reported cases over the years of a child having this kind of cancer. However, there have been five cases of children with this kind of cancer that have been reported within the past year. I have not yet been able to study exactly what these five children have in common, but it's highly unusual that there would be five children with a disease that has only affected fewer than 100 children over the course of many years."

"What would cause a cluster like this?" I asked him. For some reason, as he spoke, my heart started to race.

"That is the question. Obviously, the children who have developed this disease have to have some kind of genetic predisposition. Some really bad luck of the draw. That's the first thing that has to be present. But beyond that, these kids obviously had to have been exposed to a significant amount of asbestos. It couldn't be just an incidental exposure, like kids playing around a rock quarry or something of the sort. No, in order for a child to get mesothelioma, exposure would have to be significant."

So, from what Dr. Ramirez was telling me, I was probably barking up the wrong tree anyway when I was going through the questions I had for Lorinda about the crayons, cosmetics, talcum powder and all of that, because even these products only showed small amounts of asbestos. I doubted very seriously that incidental exposure to any one of these products would cause a disease. At least not a disease that typically shows up 40 years after the exposure.

"I'm really glad I came to see you," I said to him. "Is this something you're looking into?"

"It is, actually. The topic of the mesothelioma cluster has just come to my attention within the past few weeks. As I said, however, I have not been able to isolate any kind of commonality between the cases. I actually was going to send my field agents out to interview the families who have children with this disease. I scheduled this for next week and they'll probably will speak with your client's son. I will tell you that there is another oddity about this cluster, and that's that the cluster is not really a cluster, necessarily. The five

The Trial

children who have been diagnosed with this disease are in all areas of the country."

"Is that unusual?"

"Somewhat. Typically when I see a disease cluster, it's individuals living close to one another. That's because typically in a case that's a cluster, there is some environmental reason for it. Perhaps the water is contaminated, or the air in a certain neighborhood is polluted. Those are just some of the scenarios I typically see in disease clusters. In this case, however, the kids live all over the country. As of now, it's a bit of a mystery. Although, instinctually, I'm drawn to the Tylenol poisoning case. Do you remember that?"

I did remember that. However, the details of what happened were escaping me. "I remember something about that. It happened in the 70s, right?"

"Early 80s. 1982, to be exact. In that case, all the victims were in the Chicago area. They had all taken Tylenol laced with cyanide. All the tainted pills had come from different pharmaceutical companies, and the victims were all in the same city, so it was ruled out that the cyanide was put into the pills during production. In the end, the theory was that the killer had taken Tylenol bottles off the shelf, contaminated them with the cyanide, and then put them back on the shelf."

"In other words, it was a murder, plain and simple," I said. "If I can remember rightly, there was another ulterior motive for doing that, wasn't there? Wasn't there something about the guy having a wife he wanted to bump off, and he wanted to poison her with a poisoned Tylenol, and he was trying to say that she was yet another victim of the Tylenol poisoning. Wasn't there something like that?"

"Actually, no. The Tylenol murders were never solved. You're probably thinking of a case that happened a few years later, in 1986, where a woman poisoned her husband with cyanide in an Excedrin, and then tainted other bottles of Excedrin with poison, to make it look like her husband died through a terrorist, like with the Tylenol terrorist, or that it was a copycat of the Tylenol murders. However, she did not get away with it, because she did not cover her tracks very well. The woman in the Excedrin case was thinking about ways to kill her husband for a long time. And, that woman, I believe her name was Stella, was a fish enthusiast, and all the bottles contaminated around the area in Washington had traces of an algae killer. Plus, her daughter testified against her. So that case was solved pretty quickly and pretty cleanly. It's entirely possible that the Tylenol murderer had a similar motive, and that one of the victims of the Tylenol murders was actually somebody who the culprit was trying to kill. But, at this moment, the case has never been solved, so nobody really knows exactly what the motive was for the poisonings."

I thought about what Dr. Ramirez was talking about and had to admit the question was high in my mind. Why was his mind going to deliberate poisoning?

"It's bringing it all back to me, but I was wondering exactly why you were thinking about this case?"

"It's just a case I'm instinctually drawn to when I'm looking at this particular mesothelioma cluster case. As I told you, however, I have not yet started my investigation, so I have no idea if the Tylenol cases are related to this one. Pay me no mind, I was just thinking out loud. I'm guilty of that probably more than I would like to admit."

I had to have a chuckle at that one. "I'm usually guilty as charged about that as well. Sometimes I'll be sitting in my office, and I'm just talking to myself for hours. But usually the reason why I'm doing that is because there's something buried in my subconscious that's trying to get out. I would be interested to know if the Tylenol case does end up being some kind of an analogous situation to what's going on here."

"I definitely will keep you apprised, especially now that I know you're representing one of the victims. How did you get involved with this case, out of curiosity?"

I told him about Regina, and about how Regina was friends with Lorinda, and just happened to run into her at a coffeehouse. "I'm going to meet the young boy tonight, and I'm also going to look around her apartment to see if there's anything that catches my eye. If I do come upon something I'm suspicious of, I'll be sure and let you know. I know that it's not always easy to find a commonality amongst disease clusters, especially if the disease cluster doesn't have a common geographic area. So I'll be happy to help you out."

"Yes, please do. Anyhow, what do you think will happen in this case?"

"I don't really know. I guess if we find out there was some kind of contamination in something in the kid's environment, I'll probably file a lawsuit. At any rate, I need to try to convince the insurance company to cover some different treatments for this kid, since radiation and chemotherapy doesn't seem to be doing anything for him. Wish me luck on that."

Dr. Ramirez smiled broadly and shook his head. "Good luck. I don't know about you, but I can't stand dealing with insurance companies. They're so narrow-minded, so unwilling to take a risk. You know that because insurance companies are so hesitant to cover experimental treatments, it's really held back research in this country. It becomes a bit of a vicious circle, really. Because insurance companies are hesitant to pay for experimental treatments, fewer patients get the treatments, which means that sometimes these treatments never get off the ground. And the pharmaceutical companies which are developing these products, they don't get as much money to fund the research for these innovations because fewer patients have access to them. If insurance companies would just get behind more innovative treatment options, then I believe we would have a lot more options available for people these days. It's about time the traditional treatment of cancer in this country move beyond radiation and chemotherapy, and into more promising avenues such as immunotherapy and gene therapy. So, I wish you luck that you can get more coverage for this child."

We spoke for another 20 minutes, just basically catching up on what was going on in each other's lives. I had some time to kill, and it seemed Dr. Ramirez was wanting to talk as well, so I enjoyed our conversation.

Then, after I left his office, I headed over to Lorinda's apartment.

Chapter Five

I GOT to Lorinda's apartment, and saw that Regina was already there. She and Lorinda were sitting on a couch, with a kid who was around seven or eight years old, in between them. When I walked in the door, Lorinda stood up, and, on her face was a smile. It seemed the smile was more genuine than the one she had on her face earlier.

Then I looked over and saw there was another kid coming out of the kitchen. The other kid looked about the same age as the first kid. He plopped down on one of the couches and promptly started to play a game.

"Come sit down," Lorinda said, pointing to a recliner leather chair. I noticed the place was small, but very tidy, with hardwood floors, fairly high ceilings and colorful throw rugs scattered about the living room. Ceiling fans cooled off the home, as this was a typical San Diego abode that did not feature central air. Especially because this apartment was so close to the beach, which tended to be much cooler than inland areas, there was not really a need for central air.

Not like Kansas City, which tended to get insufferably hot in the summertime, and central air was always a must.

I sat down in the recliner chair catercorner to the sofa where Regina and Lorinda were sitting. The little boy sitting between them was very slight, and dark-haired, and was eating a bowl of ice cream. His hair was matted with sweat, and he was very pale, but, other than that, he did not necessarily look like he was sick.

I wondered if this was Frankie.

"Frankie," Lorinda said to the kid. "This is Avery. She's the woman I talked to you about. She's the one who is hopefully going to be able to help us. And that other little boy, who's sitting over there playing a video game, is Eric."

When she said that, Eric nodded and returned to his game.

Frankie nodded his head towards me and then shyly got up from the couch and politely extended his hand towards mine. "Miss Avery, I'm sorry what's your last name?" he said in a voice that was hollow and quiet, as if it was a great effort for him to verbalize the words.

"Collins," I said.

"Ms. Collins, thank you for coming to meet me. My mom told me that you might be able to help me not be so sick. I hope you can, because I don't like being sick. I don't like seeing my mom crying all the time, and I'm scared. I'm very scared."

I felt a lump in my throat for this polite and sweet little boy. It was then that I heard a slight rasp in his breath. It appeared to me that he really could not take a deep enough breath, which was why he was so pale and frail. I wondered if he was in heart failure.

He sat back down on the couch, and Lorinda put a

The Trial

hand on his chest, quietly got an oxygen tank, and hooked him up to it. "Frankie was well enough to get out of bed, but he tires out very easily," she explained. "It's just a matter of time before I have to make sure he's getting oxygen. But I'm really happy that you could come here and meet him. I think it's important you put a face to your client. I think that it helps him become more than just a number, not that he ever would be." She tousled his hair and then kissed his forehead lightly. "You're burning up, kid."

He weakly nodded, and then returned to his bowl of ice cream. "It's the one thing about being sick that's good," he said to me. "Mom lets me eat ice cream whenever I want. And pizza, too. In fact, there's a pizza coming tonight."

As if on cue, there was a knock at the door, and a guy bearing the pizza was standing there. Apparently, they had ordered a pizza from a place called Filippi's in Pacific Beach, one of my favorite Italian places, and one of my favorite pizzas. Lorinda got up and paid him, and then brought the pizza over to the table and opened it up. "This is Frankie's favorite pizza, sausage and black olives. It's been so long since he's been feeling good enough to eat pizza that I figured I would get him exactly what he wanted."

I couldn't help but think that Lorinda was overcompensating, probably because she felt Frankie was in his last days. And, looking at him, I did not doubt that was true. My heart went out to him and Lorinda. It didn't seem fair that a young boy of this age would be dying of an adult's disease, and I wondered exactly what caused it and why was Dr. Ramirez so fixated on the Tylenol tampering case. What was it about that case that got him going? How was it related to this case?

After dinner, Regina did the dishes and I took a look

around the apartment. I looked at every product in the home and didn't see anything that looked suspicious to me. She showed me her face powder, which was an organic face powder she found on Amazon. "I just don't like it when chemicals are going into my body," she explained.

Just like she said, there was no talcum powder, there were no crayons except for Crayola, no magic kits. I went into Frankie's bedroom and carefully examined all the toys neatly put into a toy box in the corner of the room. There were *Star Wars* figurines, and some Marvel comic figurines as well, such as Iron Man, The Hulk and Captain America. There also was a collection of toy cars - Porsches, Maseratis, Lamborghinis and Ferraris.

What there wasn't was anything powdered in any way.

I thought about what Dr. Ramirez told me, that the exposure to the asbestos had to be severe, and not incidental, and, while I wanted to ask Lorinda if I could have the toys tested, at the same time, I doubted these tests would bear any kind of fruit.

I saw an inhaler on the nightstand and I pointed to it. It was an inhaler designed just for children, as it was round and had a clown's face painted on it. "Is that an inhaler he uses now because of his issues with breathing?" I asked her.

She shook her head. "No, he's had asthma for most of his life. I blame myself, because when he was a baby, I smoked in the house. I didn't know it at the time, I was dumb, but my pediatrician did tell me that when you smoke around infants, you can cause asthma when the kids get a little bit older. I don't know why that inhaler is still on the nightstand because he hasn't used it in months. I guess I just haven't really bothered to clean up his room so much. Anyhow, why do you ask about it?"

The Trial

"No reason." I had looked on the Internet and could see no reason why an inhaler would be related to asbestos. However, I did notice this was a dry powder inhaler, which was a little bit different from other kinds of inhalers which uses liquid droplets. "How many dosages does an inhaler like this contain?"

"Around 50."

"And do you pick them up one at a time?"

"No, typically I pick up three months worth at any given time."

"Are they all in the same package?"

"Yes."

I picked up the inhaler, and, for some reason, I decided I really wanted to take it. "He doesn't need this anymore?"

"No, he doesn't use an inhaler anymore. He uses oxygen, but not an inhaler. So, yes, you can take that. But I don't understand why you necessarily want it."

"I don't know why, either," I said, honestly. "It's not like inhalers are ever a source of asbestos. I've heard of no cases online where any inhaler has ever tested positive for asbestos. Nevertheless, I'm curious about it. So thanks for letting me borrow it."

"Not a problem. Anyhow, do you see anything else in this apartment that has set in your hair on fire?" she asked.

"Not yet. It's still a mystery, but I'm going to see if there's anything else I can look at and possibly test. I'd like to take your cosmetics and have those tested as well. Do you mind?"

"No, I don't mind. I'll do anything to help my son get well."

By the time I left her apartment, I had a small bag of things I hoped to have examined. They consisted of the inhaler, a small vial of face powder, and, just for kicks, a candle burning in the living room. I had never heard of a candle being a source of asbestos, but there was nothing else I could really figure out that might've been the culprit.

As far as I was concerned, it was still a mystery.

But it was a mystery I was determined to solve.

Chapter Six

THE NEXT DAY, I took a close look at the Blue Cross/Blue Shield policy Lorinda had taken out on Frankie. It had some pretty boilerplate language about experimental procedures and what is and is not covered. Namely, the experimental procedures that were covered by this policy were procedures that had some kind of scientific backing to them. I read the boilerplate language, and the only experimental treatments covered had to show they were both medically necessary and were backed up by scientific studies.

After I read the policy, I spent the rest of the day looking into alternative treatments for what Frankie had. The bad thing about it was that there were absolutely no studies for Frankie's disease, childhood mesothelioma. How could there be studies on his disease when less than 100 children had ever been affected by it in the history of medicine? Of course there were no studies that would help guide the insurance company. I had a feeling that because there were no studies about the alternative treatments for mesothelioma as applied to children, which there would not be, that would be enough excuse for Blue Cross/Blue Shield to use to deny any and all claims for the treatments.

It was going to have to be up to me to try to make the argument on behalf of Frankie. I didn't think I could convince anybody, but I was going to have to try, and the first thing I would have to do was give a call to my friend who worked as a claims adjuster for the company. She was actually a friend of Regina's, and she was my contact person at this particular insurance company.

Michelle Wilson was her name and I called her office and made an appointment to see her. She was one of the leading claims adjusters. I didn't think she was necessarily the person behind denying Frankie, but she had some kind of pull over there, and if I could convince her, then probably I could get the treatment covered. At any rate, my visit with her would hopefully help her see that Frankie was not just a number.

AT 2 O'CLOCK THE next day, I was in Michelle's office. She was knee-deep in paperwork, as claims adjusters usually are, because I knew they had to process thousands of claims every day. I had a feeling Frankie was denied in a very cursory way. Probably what happened was that the claim came through and the adjuster working the case saw there were no studies to back up any of the treatment programs, and they just marked it "denied."

"Avery," she said when I walked in the door. "I saw you were meeting with me and I can't say I'm unhappy to see you. In fact, you might be just the person that I want to talk to."

The Trial

I opened my mouth to say something, but she continued on.

"I know you're here to talk about Frankie Jamison. I reviewed his file, and I have to already say that it's going to be very difficult to get me to go to bat for him. He's been receiving chemotherapy and radiation treatments, and now his mother wants us to pay for different therapies. But there are no studies backing up whether or not these treatments will be effective, so there's nothing we can do. Our hands are tied."

I took a deep breath, trying to calm down the anger building inside of me. "Here's one of the factors I know you look at in determining whether or not the claim is to be denied or approved. And that factor is that the options have been exhausted. And, as I noted, the chemotherapy and the radiation treatments Frankie has been receiving have not been effective. At all. They have not been shrinking the tumors attacking his heart, they have not alleviated any of his symptoms, they've done nothing but torture the poor kid. Now I find it incredibly cynical that your company would deny treatment that could possibly help this kid just because there's been no studies done. Of course there's been no studies done. There have been less than 100 children ever diagnosed with mesothelioma. In the history of medicine. Let alone any studies that have been done on the efficacy of treatments on Frankie's particular kind of cancer, which is the most rare one of all of them. So, no, of course there's not going to be any studies your insurance company can look at. But there are plenty of studies that have been done about the efficacy of different promising treatments on mesothelioma in adults."

At that, I gave her a stack of some of the studies I had printed out off the Internet that talked about different kinds of therapy. There were 20 different studies about immunotherapy, which included cancer vaccines, adoptive cell transfer procedures, immune checkpoint inhibitors, and monoclonal antibodies. I gave her studies about gene therapy, with gene transfer leading the way. I gave her several studies about epigenetic therapy, which was similar to gene therapy, except that it changes the DNA expression as opposed to altering the DNA sequence. All of these alternative therapies were promising, and any one of them would give Frankie a fighting chance.

"Here are the studies you need to look at. Yes, they're all on adults. The reason why they're all on adults is because it's mainly only adults that get this. Listen, if insurance companies won't cover experimental procedures for children with this disease, resigning them to just traditional therapies, then no kids are going to ever recover from this disease. You have to take a chance. The only way medicine ever progresses is when insurance companies like your insurance company takes the chance. Take the risk. Just imagine the good press the doctors will get if one of these therapies actually works for Frankie. There could very well be a Nobel Prize in the offing. And think about the good PR your insurance company can reap if it's known that the only reason why this treatment went through was because your company decided to go the humanitarian route and do the right thing. And, there's another aspect of this, and that's that there has been a small cluster of children who have been diagnosed with this disease. I have been in touch with an epidemiologist who is a friend of mine, his name is Dr. Ramirez, and he told me there have been five children diagnosed with this disease just within the past year. Which is pretty remarkable considering that prior to this, there have been fewer than 100. That means there is a cluster of children, and if there can be a helpful therapy for all of these kids, that could be another feather in your cap. At any rate, your insurance company can be a hero to not just Frankie, but to all the other kids who have been diagnosed with this dread disease. Or, alternatively, I can tell the press that you and your company have been denying potentially life-saving treatment to these kids."

I could see in Michelle's face that she was getting angry with me. She knew the PR implications for denying treatments that could save his life, and the lives of the other children, could be disastrous. It was one thing that they denied a single child potentially life-saving treatments. It would be quite another to be denying a child this life-saving treatment, which might also do good for other kids who had the same disease. Especially because this disease was so rare and the results of the treatment might be groundbreaking.

"Why isn't she pursuing a clinical trial?" she demanded.

"There's not going to be a clinical trial for something like this. Why would a researcher conduct a clinical trial for a disease that has affected so few children over the years, and who would be the subjects of this trial?"

"You just told me there was a cluster of kids who have been diagnosed with this. A good researcher might be able to conduct a clinical trial with these other children."

"I don't believe there are enough children, even now, for a clinical trial. At any rate, there are no clinical trials being conducted for children of Frankie's age for this disease. If you deny him experimental therapies, then he'll die. Plain and simple as that. He's at the end of his rope, because no traditional treatments have done anything for him whatsoever."

She crossed her arms and glared at me. "Because there've been no studies on the efficacy of these treatments on children, these treatments might very well kill him, or harm him further. Do you not understand that?"

"Of course I understand that. I also understand that, without the treatment, he's going to die anyway. Yes, I agree. There is a possibility a treatment that has not been studied on children could very well make him sicker or kill him. But when there is almost 100% chance he's going to die without any kind of experimental treatment, what do we have to lose?"

"And there are doctors who are willing to try these experimental therapies on Frankie?"

"You know there are. My client has found several doctors eager to try immunotherapy, gene therapy and all the rest. I've seen the doctors' notes. I have not yet talked to the doctors, but I've seen their notes in Frankie's file. You have too. You have those medical records as well. So you know there are several doctors who believe these treatments would be beneficial to Frankie. They are ready and willing, but they just need the insurance coverage to pay for it. Believe me, if my client had the money to pay for these treatments on her own, she would be. She's spoken with all the doctors and she's convinced these treatments will help him. So, yes, there are doctors willing and able to treat Frankie with these innovative technologies. You have the studies, you have the medical records, you have everything you need. Now I know that yours won't be the final word as to whether or not Frankie gets covered for these treatments, but I also know that your word carries a lot of weight around here. That's why I came to you first."

"These treatments are going to set us back hundreds of thousands of dollars. You understand that, right?"

I took a deep breath. "What I understand is that the public in general holds insurance companies in very low

The Trial

regard. Believe me, everybody knows that insurance companies do anything, try every trick in the book, not to have to cover illnesses. We all know stories from people who talk about how insurance companies screwed them over. Stories about people whose insurance policies are canceled when they make a large claim, such as trying to get coverage for cancer. Stories about how coverage is denied because of a technical error on the billing form. Before the Affordable Care Act came into existence, insurance companies denied large claims because the insured had a minor medical issue in her past that she forgot about, therefore did not disclose. Like not covering cancer because the insured forgot about a plantar's wart she had taken off of her foot when she was 12 years old. Everybody knows insurance companies look at their bottom line, first and foremost, finding any which way to deny claims while paying their executives exorbitant amounts of money. Believe me, your industry in general could use some good PR. And that's exactly what you will get if you cover Frankie and maybe even cover some of the other kids who have the same disease if they're under your policy. Just think about that. Yes, it will be hundreds of thousands of dollars, but that's a drop in the bucket."

She finally just took a deep breath and sat back in her chair. "It's not up to me. But I will do what I can to see that Frankie gets coverage for immunotherapy and gene therapy, on one condition - I want you to let it be known that we did this for him. I would like his case to be publicized in the New York *Times*, I know you have some contacts over there, and I want there to be several paragraphs talking about how our company was willing to go the extra mile to make sure he got coverage. I think it's a newsworthy story, especially since there's a small cluster of kids with the same disease now. So that's what I want you to do. Use your contacts over at the New York *Times*, get this in there and talk us up. Make sure everybody knows that most insurance companies would not cover these treatments for him, but we did. You do that for me and I'll go to bat for you."

I didn't like her terms, just because I didn't know how Lorinda was going to feel about the publicity that was going to come from this. Despite the fact that she was an exotic dancer, I really got the impression that she was a very private person. At the same time, however, if these were the terms, these were the terms. Michelle was definitely going out on a limb for me, so I was going to have to do the same for her. I was quite sure that if Lorinda was given the choice between Frankie not getting treatment, and dying, and Frankie getting treatment, possibly living, but having his case splashed in the New York *Times*, Lorinda would choose the latter option.

"Okay. You have a deal. And you're right, this is a newsworthy story, considering how rare this disease is."

As I left her office, I could not possibly anticipate just how newsworthy the story was going to turn out to be.

Chapter Seven

LORINDA

LORINDA HAD JUST TALKED to Avery, and, while she was ecstatic, over the moon, that Frankie was going to be able to get experimental treatments, right away, she was apprehensive about the terms. But, she agreed to them, of course. She was not going to look a gift horse in the mouth.

She didn't like the fact that there was going to be a reporter for the New York *Times* coming to her house that afternoon. She hoped the reporter would not make a big deal about her profession. She hoped the reporter would just focus on Frankie. She didn't really know why the whole topic was newsworthy in the first place, except for that Avery's friend, Dr. Ramirez, had found other kids who had the same thing. She knew the reporter was going to do some digging on these other kids as well.

It was somewhat comforting that the story was not going to be completely on Frankie. It was going to be an investigative story on these other kids and this highly unusual disease. The reporter was eager to jump on it, because apparently the media had not caught on yet that this was happening. Granted, nobody quite knew just why it was happening. Dr. Ramirez was still investigating it. But, with the help of the reporter, they could probably find out what the culprit was. What the commonality was between all the kids.

The reporter came over and spent about two hours talking to her about Frankie, and he talked to Frankie some, as well. Frankie wasn't doing well, could barely keep his eyes open, he couldn't get out of bed, and he was hooked up to oxygen, but he could talk to the reporter some, so he did.

Then the reporter left, leaving Lorinda his business card.

After he left, Lorinda went into Frankie's room, where, as usual, he was laying in bed, hooked up to his oxygen tank. On the day that Avery came to visit, Frankie actually had a good day. He was out of bed that day, at least for a few hours. He was able to eat solid food. He tired out very easily, of course, but just the fact that he was able to sit on the couch with her and Regina and eat some pizza, meant everything to Lorinda.

She went over to the bed, and smoothed back Frankie's dark hair. He opened his eyes, but just barely, and Lorinda knew it took a great deal of energy just for him to do that. "Frankie, we're going to the hospital."

He looked at her dully, and then shrugged his shoulders. "Why? I was in the hospital before, for months, and I just got sicker and sicker. That's why I'm here at home. I thought everybody had just given up."

It broke Lorinda's heart to hear Frankie talk like that. She didn't know that he was so perceptive that he knew that everybody had just given up on him. He knew he had come home to die. Chemotherapy treatment after chemotherapy treatment, radiation treatment and radiation treatment, and

The Trial

nothing was working. She felt she had put him through a torture chamber for nothing.

Was this just going to be fresh torture for him? She had no idea. She did know that the doctors treating Frankie were recommending these new treatments. And now, finally, he was going to be getting them.

Was it too late? The doctors seemed to think it was not too late, otherwise they would not be accepting him into this program for this treatment. But he was going to have to stay in the hospital while he was getting this treatment, because they were going to have to monitor him closely. That was the one thing Lorinda did not like about what was about to happen. She didn't like the fact that he was going to not be in his bed anymore, was not going to be around Eric anymore. Frankie and Eric had grown pretty close, sharing a bedroom. Frankie also was comfortable here. This was his home. And now he was going back into the sterile hospital to be poked and prodded again.

Lorinda closed her eyes and prayed for guidance. That would be the worst thing, if she put him through this again, the torture and the poking and prodding. The pain. And then he still died. She wondered if she could ever forgive herself if that happened.

But it was a chance, no matter how small. There was no way she w not going to take this opportunity, especially because Avery went through such lengths to make sure that this opportunity was even presented to her.

She smoothed his hair back again, feeling that it was wet with sweat, as it usually was. "No, honey, I never gave up on you. It was just the doctors had come to the end of the line with their treatments, and you weren't getting better. But now there's something new. I wasn't able to pay for it before, but now I can. Your insurance company is going to pay for it. So, kiddo, you have a chance to get well. I have a chance to see my boy outlive me. We're going to take that chance. I'm sorry you have to go back into the hospital. I wish I could just have you here and have you go through treatments, but these are really new treatments, and the doctors don't really know how you're going to react to them. So you have to be in the hospital so they can monitor you."

Frankie just shrugged. Lorinda knew he was too weak to do anything else but that small gesture. "Okay, Mom, let's go."

At that, Lorinda made sure Frankie was dressed in a pair of jeans and a T-shirt and tennis shoes, and she packed a small bag with everything that Frankie would need while he was in the hospital – toothbrush, toothpaste, several changes of underwear, a few of his *Star Wars* toys, and some of his favorite books – and the two of them headed over to the University of California-San Diego Medical Center on the La Jolla campus, where Frankie was going to spend the next several weeks, maybe months.

Chapter Eight

AVERY

I WAS HAVING dinner with Regina and my brother, Aidan, at my house, when I got the phone call from Dr. Ramirez. The phone call a good distraction for me because I was getting kind of sick of seeing Regina and Aidan canoodle at the dinner table. They were clearly smitten with each other, and I knew it was a long time coming, because I always knew Aidan had a mad crush on her, but I didn't think Regina would fall so hard for him.

I tried to silence the inner voice that was telling me the reason I was uncomfortable watching Regina and Aidan together was because my own love life was perpetually in the toilet. Yes, I was working all the time. But I really didn't have to work all the time. I didn't have to bust my tail for every last dime. The settlement from the state of Missouri for my false imprisonment would carry me through the rest of my life. But I did work a lot, and I was probably going to have to go into therapy to find out exactly why I worked so much. What was driving me to put work in front of any kind of personal life? If it wasn't for the money, what was it?

These existential questions were going to have to be answered a little bit later, because Dr. Ramirez was calling me at home. That had to mean that whatever he was going to say to me was somewhat urgent.

"Hey, Dr. Ramirez," I said to him. "How are you?"

"I'm sorry to bother you at home. But can you possibly come into my office? I did my preliminary investigation of the children who have come down with this disease and I found some interesting commonalities. I could certainly talk to you about this over the phone, but I'd rather see you face-to-face. Is that possible?"

I looked over at Regina and Aidan, both of whom looked like they would not even notice if I left anyhow, and nodded. "Of course, I'll come down to your office. I'm very curious about what you found."

"I'll see you soon."

I hung up the phone and looked over at Regina. "That was Dr. Ramirez. You remember I told you that he was noticing a small cluster of children who had come down with the same disease as Frankie? When I saw him, he told me he had not yet begun his investigation to find the commonalities. But he just called me and it sounds like maybe he has it figured out. At least, on a preliminary basis. So I need to talk to him and see what he found out."

Regina looked at Aidan. "Can I come with you?"

"Of course. You're the investigator on this case. Plus I would not have the case if not for you. But you don't have to. Maybe you just want to stay here with Aidan, walk on the beach and hang out."

I could see in Aidan's eyes that that's exactly what he wanted to do. He looked at Regina like a puppy dog. However, I only noticed him looking at her like that when her attention was turned elsewhere or her back was turned. He knew, as well as I did, that the only reason why they were working was because Regina did not know the depth of his emotion for her. So he always tried to play it cool around her. But I knew he was mooning over her all the time.

"Nah, I can walk on the beach with Aidan anytime I want," Regina said. "I mean, this guy called you at home, asked to see you right away. Obviously, he has some kind of information and I want to know what that is. I want to ask him questions. So I know Aidan won't mind if I come with you."

Aidan didn't say anything, which, to me, spoke volumes. I had a feeling that spending the evening alone with Regina was exactly what he wanted to do.

"Aidan?" I said to him.

"Yeah. Go on, Regina. I'll be here when you get back."

So Regina and I headed over to Dr. Ramirez's office.

"What do you think he is going to say to us?" Regina asked.

"I don't really know. But, whatever he's going to say, it's going to help us in our case."

"By the way," Regina said. "I meant to tell you that you did really an awesome job with that stupid insurance company. I talked to Lorinda and she told me Frankie was in the hospital and he's gone through several rounds of treatment already. She said his numbers are getting better, by a lot. She also said he's been out of his hospital bed just about every day, watching TV, walking around the hallways, eating solid food, and gaining weight. That's all just within the past few days. It sounds like this treatment is finally working. It sounds like he might get better, finally. So, if he beats this thing, goes into remission, it's going to be because of you."

That made me feel good. Sometimes things happened that made it all worth it. This was one of those things. "I'm going to have to go see him in the hospital. In the meantime, I'm really anxious to find out just what Dr. Ramirez found. I wonder if it'll help Frankie's doctors in treating him."

We got to Dr. Ramirez's office and he stood up. I looked at the clock, realizing it was 8 o'clock at night, and I wondered if he ever slept. "Avery, Regina, it's so good to see both of you," he said to us as we walked in his office. "Sit down, sit down."

We took a seat and waited for him to tell us what was going on.

"Okay, here's what I found. I interviewed all the family and friends of the other five children who have been diagnosed with the same mesothelioma as Frankie. Actually, I should probably amend that. The other kids have mesothelioma, but not all of them have pericardial. Some have pleural, some have peritoneal. But they all have mesothelioma. And other doctors have found out our office is studying this cluster, and I have discovered that there are 14 more cases around the world. So it seems as if a disease that has previously affected less than 100 children ever in the history of medicine has suddenly afflicted almost 20 children just within the past few months. I have interviewed, or I've had my staff interview, the families around these new cases as well. There was only one thing in common I saw in all these patients."

"What is that?" I asked, feeling my heart started to race. It seemed I was going to get the answer to the intriguing question I had about how Frankie would've been exposed to asbestos in the amount that he would need to be exposed to in order to get this disease at such a young age.

"All of the children were prescribed a dry-powder inhaler. Furthermore, all of the dry-powder inhalers prescribed to these kids were dry-powder inhalers marketed especially to children. In other words, they were inhalers designed to look like little smiley faces or little elephants or something of the sort."

I thought about what he was saying and what that implied. "I don't understand. I did my research on this matter, and I never have seen that asthma inhalers have been a source of asbestos."

"You're right about that. And that's because the research on asbestos shows the products that contain asbestos contain it in an incidental way. That means it's more or less accidental. For instance, talcum powder contains asbestos because talc is mined in areas contaminated with asbestos in the rocks where talc is procured. The chemicals in crayons can also be contaminated by asbestos for the same reason. At any rate, in the cases of crayons, talcum powder, magic kits, every other source of asbestos the child might come into contact with – the asbestos in these products is incidental and, clearly, not placed there deliberately."

I looked over at Regina, who was looking back at me with a bewildered look on her face that said *who the hell would deliberately poison kids with asbestos?*

"Go on. Tell me what you're thinking."

"Well, I was able to have every single one of the dry powder inhalers tested in a lab. And every one of them came back positive for asbestos. The powder in these inhalers were tested as 20% asbestos powder. Bear in mind that asbestos does not have a smell, so there would be no way these parents would know what they were giving their child. But I can only conclude one thing – these inhalers were sabotaged. I've already alerted the FDA and they have agreed to initiate a recall of all dry powder inhalers, just to be safe. However, I did notice another thing – every single one of the dry powder inhalers that I tested, that came back positive for asbestos, came from the same manufacturer and the same factory."

"Who was the manufacturer?"

"It's a small company called Columba. They have a factory located in El Cajon. Only one factory. However, even though they're small by the standards of most pharmaceutical companies, they have a decent amount of annual sales. They do about a billion in sales a year. The name of the inhalers, the drugs that are supposed to be administered through these dry powder inhalers, is Spiritus."

I suddenly realized Dr. Ramirez' earlier hunch about sabotage had come to fruition. There was a reason his intuition was drawn towards the Tylenol scare – just like with that case, apparently in this case, there was some kind of terrorist at work. This was going to induce panic in this country, as parents across the country realize the dry powder inhalers they were giving their children might have pure poison inside of them. I also thought about the vaping crisis, where hundreds of people have gotten sick or had died because of apparently contaminated E-cigarettes. So far, there have been no culprits found for the vaping crisis, although I suspected deliberate contamination in that case as well.

"Tell me your theory of the case."

"One caveat. I don't know any kind of motive for why anybody would do this," Dr. Ramirez cautioned. "I have suspected all along that something nefarious was behind this cluster of kids getting this disease, just because in order for child to get a disease such as this, the exposure to asbestos would have to be stratospheric. And when you replace dry powder in an inhaler with 20% asbestos, this would be enough exposure for a child to get mesothelioma, assuming the child has some kind of genetic proclivity for the disease. I never thought the kids were being exposed incidentally, like eating crayons or something of the sort. That was why my mind was immediately drawn to sabotage, and the reason why I immediately thought about the Tylenol scare. The Tylenol scare, as we were talking about, was a terroristic act. It's the best known act of its kind, where there was killing people through sabotage in an everyday product. There was no known motive in that case, simply because it has never been solved. And, in the end, there might not be a motive for the Tylenol poisonings. The culprit could've just been a psychotic person who wanted to do something like that just because. So in this case I have not even begun to work out a motive for why somebody would do something like this."

"I understand, but just tell me your theory."

"Let's just go through the facts. All the children who have been exposed to asbestos were exposed to it through an inhaler designed especially for children. A lot of children use inhalers identical to the ones adults use. This was not the case here. Because these inhalers were designed to appeal to children – they had smiley faces painted on them, they had elephants and clowns painted on them, etc. – I can only assume the person who sabotaged these inhalers was targeting specifically children. That said, my investigators are fanned out, trying to find out if any adult inhalers have been affected. It could be that the only reason we have discovered the children's inhalers have been affected by this asbestos is because so few children are identified with the disease that it's fairly easy to find a commonality. However, since thousands of adults are identified with the disease every year, it's not nearly so easy to find a commonality between the adults. It's entirely possible there are some adults who got this disease through their inhalers as well. Therefore, my inspectors are identifying anybody who has gotten an inhaler through this company, and they are discreetly going to these individuals and inquiring with them to see if they could test their inhalers."

"And have you been able to test any of the adults' inhalers?"

"We have. And, so far, none of the adult inhalers that are dry powder and have been manufactured by this company have tested positive for asbestos. Only the children's."

I took a deep breath. "So, as of now, your best theory is that this is a sabotage targeting exclusively children. Is that what you're thinking?"

"Yes, that's definitely what I'm leaning towards. Now why it would be that the sabotage would be exclusively targeting children, I do not know. Nor do I necessarily know exactly what went wrong at the Columba facility. I do know there will be a panic when this gets out, and there's a possibility that even more children have been affected. There is also a possibility that some children have been exposed to this asbestos but have not yet been diagnosed with mesothelioma. Bear in mind that it's still unusual for children to be diagnosed with mesothelioma, even when they're exposed to it as such high levels as in these inhalers. As I was saying earlier, the children who get this disease have to have some kind of genetic predisposition to it that's exacerbated by their exposure to asbestos. So we might be looking at thousands of cases down the line of kids who get mesothelioma when they are adults because of this."

"Well," Regina said. "Looks like this has made our case a lot easier. We slap a lawsuit on these bastards, they settle with us, and that's it. It's pretty open and shut that poor Frankie got sick because of his inhaler. Thank God the kid is getting real treatment now. They were poisoning him with all that chemo and radiation. All along, they could have been using that immunotherapy, the stuff that's working on him, but his cheap-ass insurance company wasn't going to do anything. Now, Avery, you've whipped the insurance company into shape. Let's go after the real bad guys."

"Regina is right," I said. "Dr. Ramirez, you certainly have made my job a lot easier. Now I know who to sue. But I wonder how easy it will be to get them to settle. Is there any way you can tell exactly how the asbestos got into these inhalers? Can you tell if it was put into the inhalers on the factory floor, as it was manufactured, or if it was put into inhalers after they had already been on the shelves?" I thought about the Tylenol case and about how the Tylenol pills were contaminated. The theory about the Tylenol capsules was that somebody had bought the Tylenol capsules, taken them home, opened up the bottles, put the cyanide into the capsules, then took the bottles back to the stores and placed them on the shelf. I knew that after this happened that companies were very careful to create tamperproof bottles, where the consumer would presumably know their bottle is safe because there was foil covering the opening.

"That's the thing with these inhalers. The way that they are created, there could be a way to tamper with them after the point-of-sale. So, theoretically, somebody would be able to buy an inhaler, take it home, put asbestos into it, and then put it back on the shelf. However, the FDA is going to be launching an investigation into the company. There certainly will be a definitive answer as to how these inhalers got contaminated. It might take months, however."

Nevertheless, I was going to file a lawsuit against the company.

Chapter Nine

AFTER OUR MEETING with Dr. Ramirez, Regina and I went back to my apartment. We were going to talk to Aidan about what we found out. I thought that maybe he could shed some light on the psychology of somebody who would do something like this. After all, Aidan's specialty, the specialized part of the law he was working in, was involuntary commitments. He worked with people who, against their will, were committed into a mental institution of some sort. As such, he was very used to dealing with people psychotic in some way. I knew one thing – the person behind this was probably psychotic. Nobody else would do such dastardly deed.

When we got into my apartment, Aidan was sitting on his bed, watching television. He smiled when he saw Regina. He patted the bed next to him, inviting Regina to join him. Regina just shook her head. "Aidan, we need to talk to you."

"What's going on?" he asked, looking at Regina and me.

He came out of his bedroom and joined us in the living room.

"Here's what we found out about what's going on with Frankie, the kid diagnosed with mesothelioma," I said. "We found out his asthma inhaler was infected with a large amount of asbestos. He had this inhaler, it had 50 doses in it, and each of these doses was comprised of 20% asbestos. Worse, he was not the only one affected by this. Obviously somebody sabotaged it, but I wanted to ask what you thought about it. Who would do something like that?"

Aidan looked a little stunned when I asked him that question. "You mean somebody was deliberately trying to make kids sick with this disease?"

"Yes. Dr. Ramirez called it a terroristic act. He seems to think the person who did it was just psycho, maybe somebody who just wanted to see the world burn. But, the strange thing is, this person just apparently targeted children. That's what's so odd. If it was somebody who was just psychotic, who just wanted to indiscriminately kill people through sabotaging their inhalers, wouldn't they target adults as well? It just seems like this guy had it out for children."

"You keep using the male pronoun," Aidan pointed out to me. "How do you know it's a man?"

"I don't know, I don't mean to. I guess I have an unconscious bias, or maybe it's a conscious one, that a woman would not do something like this to children. But you're right – it could very well be a woman who did it. Man, or woman, who would do something so terrible?"

Aidan tapped his fingers on the coffee table in front of him. "I'm just going to throw shit out there. I'm just going to spitball it. But maybe the person you need to look for is somebody who lost a child. Somebody who feels that life has treated them unfairly, so they want to spread their pain around to other people. Somebody who feels that if somebody else is suffering, that means the world is a bit more fair."

"You know, " Regina said. "Aidan might be onto something here. What if the person who did it was somebody who lost their child to this disease? I mean, think about it. There have been less than 100 children ever in the history of medicine to have gotten this disease. It's that rare. Think about how easy it would be to figure out who in the Columba company might have had a kid who died of this disease. All we need to do is find the 100 kids who have died of this disease, find out who their families are, and then see if any member of their families worked at the Columba plant. I could certainly see a person who lost their kid to a disease that was this rare wanting to spread it around so they don't feel so alone in the world."

"That's sick," I said. "Your kid dies of a rare disease and you want other kids to die of that same rare disease? That doesn't make any sense."

Regina sighed. "Don't you know by now, after all the criminals you have defended, that the criminal mind doesn't often make a lot of sense? If you ask me, this motivation is understandable. Not rational, not right, but I could see it."

Regina was right about that. There was nothing rational about some people's brains. That was true about most of my clients.

"Okay, Regina, that's what I want you to do. Maybe you could get together with Dr. Ramirez tomorrow and the two of you could go through the list of the 100 kids who have been infected with the disease prior to this latest cluster.

Then you can match up employees of Columba, to see if there's anybody who was working for Columba who might've had a child who died of this disease."

The next day, Regina did exactly that.

Chapter Ten

REGINA

REGINA WENT to see Dr. Ramirez the day after she talked to Avery about this case. "Hey, Doc, I put my head together with Avery and her brother, Aidan, and we came up with a good idea. We decided that it would be smart to look at all the kids who died of mesothelioma in the past, since there were so few of them, and see if we could find anybody who had a kid who died who also works for the Columba plant. Aidan's theory is that maybe somebody who had a kid who died from it wants other kids to die from it, too."

Dr. Ramirez shook his head. "That's completely twisted, but I suppose it's not outside the realm of possibility. At any rate, I was already working on just that. I, too, thought that maybe the person who was killing these kids, or making them sick, might've been somebody who had been touched by the disease. That's the only motivation I can see for infecting kids with such a specific illness, and such a deadly one. I did come up with a name. There was one person, about two years ago, whose child, Aurora, died of the disease. His name is Andrew Garvey. He's an inspector at the plant, the last inspector these inhalers go through. I don't know for sure, but if he did it, I would imagine that he added in the asbestos into the inhalers right before he gave them the seal of approval. I have already notified the FBI and they're going to speak with him tomorrow."

Regina didn't know how she felt about the fact that the FBI was already on the case. She wanted to talk to him directly and she might not get the chance to do that. Then again, the FBI could do the dirty work, and she could just piggyback off them. "You sure the FBI is going to talk to him tomorrow?"

"Yes. They were skeptical about my theory, but they also didn't believe it was necessarily coincidence that somebody who lost a child to a very rare disease would be the same person working in the factory where the contaminated inhalers originated from. I'm a firm believer that there are no coincidences. I'm not saying the FBI will make an arrest. They don't have probable cause for that. But they're going to talk to him."

Regina knew she would have to talk to him before the FBI got to him. Once the FBI started their investigation, it could be difficult to get information from them. Regina had found that FBI agents were extremely tightlipped in their investigations while the investigations were going on. And she just had the feeling she could break him down if she just saw him. "What time are the FBI agents going to talk to him, do you know?"

"No. Probably in the afternoon. Why?"

"Because I want to talk to him. Before the agents get a chance at him. The manufacturer's factory is in El Cajon, right?"

"Yes. I don't necessarily think you're going to be able to get on the factory floor to talk to him, however. But maybe you will. After all, you have a Private Investigator license. Anyhow, I wish you luck. I just hope they don't decide to stonewall you."

REGINA ACTUALLY THOUGHT BETTER about going up to the factory to speak with Andrew. She thought it might be easier to wait until the FBI spoke with him, and then, after Avery filed her case against Columba, Avery would have a right to discovery on the case. She presumably would be able to get the information from the FBI about this Andrew Garvey character.

As curious as Regina was about why Andrew, if he was the one who actually sabotaged the inhalers, would do such a thing, she ended up thinking it was not good to step on the FBI's toes.

Chapter Eleven

AVERY

IT HAD BEEN two weeks since the FBI questioned Andrew Garvey about the sabotage of the dry powder inhalers. He denied everything and the agents did not have enough to charge him. I had filed my case against Columba, and I was in contact with the lawyers for all the other children sickened by the Columba inhalers. I found out that not every child had been as lucky as Frankie, who really was making a remarkable turnaround ever since the doctors had started him on rounds of immunotherapy treatments. In fact, Lorinda had called me to tell me that Frankie was home from the hospital and was going to continue his treatment on an outpatient basis.

"He's like a different boy. He actually has energy to watch television with me and joke around like he used to. We've been playing board games together and he's taught me the rules of his favorite video game. Before he got sick, he was interested in joining the swim team, and now he's talking about it again. Avery, he has not even been in school for the past year, and he's not only anxious to get back to school, but he's looking forward to living a normal life. We're going trick or treating on Halloween, which is tomorrow. He's going as Iron Man. It cost me a mint for that costume, I'll tell you that, but I was thrilled to pay it."

I smiled. "You'll have to send me pictures of him in his Iron Man costume," I said. "Where are you taking him?"

"To the fancy neighborhoods in Del Mar. It's a good drive, but, hey, I'm trick or treating with my kid. I'll take him wherever he wants to go."

"Good luck. He'll probably get some pretty good stuff in those neighborhoods."

"He will." She paused and I could tell she was near tears. "I'm sorry, but I've just been so emotional lately. I just can't believe my kid actually might turn a corner. I have you to thank for it too. If you didn't go to bat for me, none of this would've ever happened. I just can't believe the insurance company would've denied our claims, would've denied my child's right to try everything under the sun to try to get well. I have you, you're my angel, but those other families don't have you in their corners. And their kids are probably going to die because maybe chemotherapy and radiation won't work with them. Maybe all the other kids need the same kind of treatment my Frankie got."

The upshot was that Frankie was getting better and he was home. I didn't dare to hope that Frankie would go into complete remission, let alone that he would be cured. But it certainly was promising.

Even more promising was the fact that after I filed the case against Columba, the first thing I did was schedule a deposition for Andrew. I was still focused on him. I was starting to be convinced, more and more, that he was the one behind the sabotage of the inhalers. The thing of it was, I had no idea *why* he was behind it. I had some ideas, and I was going to ask him.

The deposition was scheduled for today. I had my court reporter ready in my conference room, I had my questions for him, and I was just waiting for him and his attorney to show up. In the meantime, Christian came down the hall to check on me and ask me what I was doing.

"Getting ready for a deposition in my Frankie Jamison case," I said. I had already briefed Christian on the facts of the case and he was interested in helping out and perhaps being my second chair for the trial. Assuming there was a trial. After the terrible publicity Columba started facing once the media got a hold of what happened with these inhalers - and the media had been all over this case ever since it was discovered what had happened with these kids – I figured it was just a matter of time before they settled. I was curious about why the lawyers had not already signaled they were ready to settle with my client, or any of the clients suing them. I knew it was early yet and the discovery process had not even really begun. Yet I knew that with the amount of press they were getting, it was in their best interest to make it all go away with confidential settlements.

"I've had my ear to the ground on this Columba thing," Christian told me. "And I've heard they're not going to settle with anybody on this case. I don't know why. I would think it would be in their best interest to settle. But maybe when you talk to this Andrew Garvey guy, you can get a handle on what's going on."

I bit my lower lip, thinking about that. I didn't like what I was hearing. I thought maybe the company had something up their sleeve, but I didn't really know what it was.

After I did my deposition with Andrew, I had my suspicions on what was going on with the company. Andrew

The Trial

answered all my questions, truthfully. A little too truthfully, and conveniently, for my taste. I got the satisfaction of him admitting he did it and I even got his motivation out of him, but I was still very suspicious something was up. A game was afoot and I didn't know exactly what kind of game it was.

"Mr. Garvey, you admitted you sabotaged the dry powder inhalers by adding asbestos into them. Right?" I asked him after a good two hours of breaking him down methodically, and finding out exactly how and why he sabotaged the inhalers.

"That's right. I did it."

"And why did you do that?" I asked him.

He took a deep breath and then looked down at his shoes. He was a big man, about 250 pounds, with dark curly hair and a very sad expression. He explained to me before the deposition ever started that, at one time, he was a fit and trim man with a family. Then his daughter, Aurora, named after the sleeping beauty, passed away, and his marriage fell apart. He fell apart, as well, and lost himself in food, gaining 100 lbs in a short period of time.

He was almost apologetic for his appearance, not that I really cared. He was fine. People gain weight for many reasons and it was not for me to judge.

"Aurora died," he said. "She died because the doctors did not know how to treat her. There are so few kids like her with this disease that nobody knew what to do to make her better. There were no studies done on children like her. And the reason why there were no studies done was because there were less than 100 cases, ever in the history of medicine. I knew that no studies would ever be done for children with mesothelioma. That's the problem when a case is such a rarity. I wanted there to be some research done on this disease. I wanted the doctors to try to find a cure for it."

It was suddenly becoming clear exactly what kind of twisted logic this guy was using. If I was to believe what he was saying, he was intimating that he wanted to make a bunch of kids sick with the disease his daughter died of, so maybe doctors and researchers would take notice of the disease and would work to find treatments for these children.

"Look at what happened here," Andrew said. "Your client, Frankie Jamison, he's been doing remarkably well with his immunotherapy treatment. This is something that is going to be so promising, because of Frankie's success, that other researchers will try it on the other kids, and if they all get better as well, it's a breakthrough. Maybe, down the line, when other kids get this disease, doctors will know what to do with them. The doctors will know what works and how to treat these kids. But that would never happen unless there was some kind of epidemic where doctors and researchers are forced to confront it."

As I sat there, listening to him make a full confession to me during our deposition, I was extremely suspicious. This was just too easy. Too pat. Here was a guy admitting to making these kids sick, deliberately, and, assuming at least some of the sickened children died, this guy would be facing murder charges. Even if the kids didn't die, he would be facing multiple criminal charges for the battery of these children. He was also going to be personally sued by each and every family of these children.

So what was his game?

The deposition concluded a few hours later, but I knew I would to have to talk to Christian and see what he thought about it. There was something weird about all this and it was bothering me. So far, the company, Columba, was not making any kind of movements toward settlement with the people affected by this. Now, here was this guy, puking up a confession like it was a day in the park. I knew that in his mind, he believed he was doing the right thing. People always do. The old saying was always true – everybody is always the hero of their own story. Everybody can justify in their mind anything they do. To me, obviously, it was a sick, sick thing what this guy was doing. But, in his mind, it was justified, because he wanted more research done on this particular disease. To himself, he was a hero in this situation.

After Andrew left my office and the court reporter had packed up and gone, I went down to Christian's office to pick his brain. I knocked lightly on his open door and he looked at me from his desk and smiled. "How did it go?" he asked.

"Weird. The guy just came in and spilled his guts. He said he sickened these kids because he wanted there to be more research done on the disease. He specifically stated that he was doing what he was doing because he wanted future generations of children to have some options if they get diagnosed with this. Why would he do this? Why would he just lay down like this? I think there's something very fishy to all of this."

"That *is* weird. I would imagine the FBI will be going over to his house today. As soon as they get a copy of the transcript from this deposition, they're going to be breaking down his door."

THE NEXT DAY, my question was answered. Andrew Garvey was found dead in his home. The time of death was apparently within an hour after he left my office. The FBI agents did in fact go to his house to question him. That's when they found him in his garage, in his car, the exhaust running.

I would have to figure out if there was a suicide note and what the suicide note said. At any rate, his suicide answered the question as to why he was so eager to come clean to me about what he did. He must've been planning this all along. He got a chance to clear his conscience and he took it.

But was it something more than that?

Chapter Twelve

I GOT the name of the FBI agent working Andrew's case and I made an appointment to talk to him about Andrew. I explained to him that I was part of a lawsuit that had Andrew at the center of it and I told him that I wanted to know if there was a suicide note, and if there was, I wanted to know the contents of it. The agent explained that the case would be closed, naturally, because Andrew was dead, and that he had no problem sharing the note with me.

So I found myself heading to the headquarters of the San Diego FBI field office. It was a 15 story tall building, with a glass façade, very modern, yet it also looked like a mid-century building. I entered the front door, showed the receptionist my California bar card, and explained who I was looking for. "I need to talk to Agent Pompeo," I explained to her. "I have an appointment."

She buzzed me through, after giving me a map of the building and explaining where I could find his office. I got to his office and knocked on the door. He answered it, shook my hand, and invited me in.

"You must be Ms. Collins," he said. "I understand that you want to talk to me about Andrew Garvey."

"Yes," I said as I sat down. "As I explained to you over the phone, I filed a lawsuit against Columba, the drug company that employed Andrew. I understand he was behind deliberately sickening 20 children, and counting. He confessed everything to me. But I wanted to find out what you knew about him."

He steepled his hands and leaned back in his chair. "We had our eye on him. Dr. Ramirez made a referral to this office. He explained what was happening with the drug company and said we should probably question him. Dr. Ramirez had a hunch that Andrew had something to do with the children being exposed to asbestos, but we questioned him, or I questioned him, and he denied everything. I didn't have anything to really go on, except for the hunch of Dr. Ramirez, and the fact that Mr. Garvey apparently had a child who died of mesothelioma. To me, that was not enough probable cause to arrest him. I had to have more. So, even though we questioned him, we released him that day. But he was still under investigation. We were looking for something more to charge him."

"And that was Tuesday of last week?"

He looked through his notes. "Yes. It was Tuesday of last week. I understand that you took his deposition last Friday. I got a copy of the deposition transcript Friday afternoon, and I saw immediately that he had confessed to putting the asbestos into the children's inhalers. Obviously that gave me probable cause to arrest him, so I headed over to his house to do just that. But, when I got there, I found out he was dead. He had committed suicide."

"And was there a suicide note?" I asked.

"There was. Here's a copy of it. The original is going

The Trial

into the file, and, as I explained to you over the phone, the file will be closed within a few weeks."

I looked at the copy of the note, which was a couple of pages long.

I, Andrew Garvey, am of sound mind and body. I am doing this for the good of all. I have been such a screwup my entire life, and this is the only good thing that I have done.
I really did believe that I was doing the right thing by planting asbestos into the inhalers of these children. 20 years down the line, there might possibly be a treatment plan for the next child who comes down with this disease, and if that child has a treatment plan, it will be because of my actions. I understand that one child coming down with this disease means that researchers and doctors will simply put up their hands and not try to come up with treatment options for children with this disease. But, when 20, 30, 40, 50, or more kids suddenly are sickened by such a rare disease, it suddenly becomes a big story. The media covers it. People take notice. Parents become scared for their own child, and there is suddenly an agitation to find a cure, and that's exactly what's happening. The New York Times has been covering this epidemic, just about every day. There has been a panic amongst all the parents who have bought an inhaler from this company for their child. Parents have been writing their representatives, demanding something be done about this. Suddenly, the topic of mesothelioma and children is a hot one.
And some of the kids have this disease are already being approved for alternative treatments. Doctors will know so much more about this disease than they ever would have if I didn't do this. So I hope every-body affected by these inhalers, through my actions, will forgive me for what I've done. I truly believe in the doctrine of utilitarianism – the best policy is one that does the most good for the most people. If there's a raging wildfire, and the government has to blow up a house to stop this fire, it's a tragedy for the person who lost their house, but, in the

end, it's a necessary evil. Because that person was willing to sacrifice their house, they end up saving hundreds of other homes. To me, my sickening these children is the same kind of necessary evil. These kids will get sick, but hundreds of other kids might be saved in the future. I wished to God that somebody would've done this years ago and maybe if they had, my Aurora would have had treatment options when she got sick. The doctors did not know what to do with her, they did not know how to treat her, so she died. I just don't want that to happen to any other kid, so I did what I did.

I am not a monster. I want everybody to know that. I'm definitely not an angel, either. I'm simply a man who saw what needed to be done to get researchers interested in fighting this disease.

Please know that I am very sorry for what I did. And I'm very sorry for taking this final act. I can only take this final act with a clear conscience, knowing nobody's life will be negatively affected by my taking my own. In fact, lots of people will actually benefit from it, including my lovely wife, Barbara, and kids with cancer.

Again, I pray that I will be forgiven for what I have done.

I read the note, again and again, and I fixated on certain phrases. He was killing himself for the good of all? What did that mean? Was I reading this correctly? It was ambiguous, in a way. Most of this note talked about how poisoning the kids was for the good of all. But it seemed that he twice mentioned the fact that him taking his own life was also for the good of all. In the first paragraph, he talked about taking his life as being for the good of all. In the second to last paragraph, he said a lot of people would benefit from him killing himself.

I looked over at Agent Pompeo. "What do you make of this? What do you make of what he's talking about when he talks about how suicide will be for the good of others?"

Agent Pompeo shook his head. "I don't know. And,

quite frankly, I don't know that I'm ever going to know. I have to close this case. I really don't want to, because, like you, I realize there are a lot of loose threads hanging. However, because resources are limited, agents are limited, we really can't afford to keep going on a case where the principal is dead. So I don't know that we will ever know exactly what he was talking about or who he was talking about when he said his suicide will benefit others."

I felt frustrated. It was very cryptic, those two phrases in the note. It was almost as if somebody was trying to reward him, somehow, for killing himself. No, not reward him, *per se*, but reward others? If so, who would that be? And who would be the ones who would be making that reward? Did somebody explicitly tell him that if he killed himself, somebody else would benefit?

"I guess that's a mystery I'm going to have to solve," I said. "At any rate, thank you very much for taking the time to talk to me about this. I appreciate you being so transparent about this, and, even though this suicide note has not really shined too much light, it's still helpful. Was there anything else he said to you when you questioned him that stood out to you? That seemed suspicious?"

"No. I've gone through my notes on my interrogation with him, and there's nothing really that stands out as being incriminating. He simply said that he had no idea what I was talking about. He seemed shocked that somebody would do such a thing as deliberately contaminate children's inhalers. He seemed especially shocked that somebody would target children at all. Now, I understand why he targeted children and not adults. In his twisted way, he really thought he was bringing about the impetus for a cure for the disease. I'm not a profiler, so I don't get too much in the weeds into the psychology of criminals, so I can't really speak to exactly what was going through his mind. It could be just what he says – he wanted researchers to take note of this disease. Or, there could be some other motivation for him doing what he did. Again, I suppose we'll never know."

I left his office feeling out of sorts. There were just too many pieces of this puzzle that were not quite fitting in.

I supposed I would eventually get the answers.

I just didn't know how much I would like those answers.

Chapter Thirteen

A COUPLE OF WEEKS LATER, some of the pieces of the puzzle managed to fit.

I got a motion to dismiss my case against Columba in the mail. And, when I read the basis for the motion to dismiss, I felt a sense of boiling rage bubbling up inside of me.

I went down to Christian's office, and, with shaking hands, I laid Columba's motion to dismiss on his desk. "I can't even believe what I'm reading. But, this motion to dismiss explains a lot. It explains why Columba has not initiated any kind of settlement talks with me or anybody else suing them. If they think they're going to get away with this, they have another thing coming."

Christian looked at the motion. "Oh. I see. They're trying to get out of having any kind of liability for this case, because their claim is that they were not negligent, and even if they were negligent, they were not the proximate cause of the children getting sick."

"Right. They're trying to claim that Andrew's criminal

acts in contaminating these dry powder inhalers is a superseding cause of the children's sicknesses."

In law, the doctrine of superseding causation meant that an individual's, or company's, negligence was not the cause of the harm, whatever the harm may be. So, in this case, they were trying to claim that because Andrew's act was a criminal act, and was not foreseeable, they were therefore off the hook. They were not the proximate cause of the children getting sick.

"Well, let's just think this through," Christian said. "This place employed a guy who criminally put asbestos powder into the dry powder inhalers of children around the country. Now, obviously, they're not going to succeed on this motion to dismiss. We can simply argue that it was their negligence that allowed this to happen in the first place. They're trying to pin 100% of the blame on Andrew for any of this happening. They know Andrew is a convenient scapegoat, considering he's dead, and, as far as we know, he's judgment-proof. As far as we know, the guy probably did not have a pot to piss in, therefore he cannot pay these claims."

"As far as we know," I echoed. "I just don't understand how they think they're going to get away with this. I mean, what kind of lax enforcement was going on over there that he was able to even do this? To me, this motion to dismiss is way premature, at the very least. I have not even gotten their discovery back, so I don't know about the inspection and enforcement they have going on over there. Perhaps that's the point. They want to try to pin all of this on the criminal who did this and not take any responsibility for their role in it."

"Case law is pretty firm on this particular point. Unfortunately, criminal acts are usually seen by courts as superseding, because it is so unforeseeable that it would happen. So, let's just say for the sake of argument that the protocols Columba used to inspect these inhalers was lax. Certainly if there was lax inspection that allowed some contaminated inhalers to go out, and these inhalers were not deliberately tampered with, in other words, there was not an intentional superseding act that caused the contamination, they would be liable for the negligence. It's certainly foreseeable that some incidental contamination would happen and their inspection practices should have caught it. What they're trying to say in this motion is that we could not foresee that somebody would deliberately tamper with these inhalers, and the fact that somebody did deliberately tamper with them, absolves them of responsibility. Personally, I think that's a bullshit argument and you need to hammer back on that aggressively."

I tapped my fingers on his desk, feeling the rage inside of me, but knowing I would have to quell it in order to think rationally about all of this. "To be superseding, both the act must be unforeseeable and the injury must be unforeseeable. We have to show the act was not unforeseeable. Yes, the guy was a criminal, and he was intentionally doing this, but was it not foreseeable that somebody would do something like that? Wasn't it foreseeable that somebody would commit a crime, seeing how they could get away with it if their enforcement mechanisms were porous?"

"Maybe, but courts have often held that intentional and criminal acts are not necessarily foreseeable. As for the injury being foreseeable, that would be a tough thing to argue as well. How could it possibly be foreseeable that children would get mesothelioma from inhaling one of their inhalers? That is so outside the realm of possibility that I can understand their argument. I'm sorry, I'm just being a devil's advocate so you know how to combat this. You're going to have to get your case law in order, and get your facts in order, and, at the very least, argue that it's way premature to dismiss this case before any discovery has been exchanged. I wish you good luck with this. Let me know if there's anything you need for me to do. I'm pretty good at research. I'm also pretty good at arguing a case. As you know. I think I can probably take this case. I could probably argue this motion to dismiss and win. I know you can too."

I looked out the window, feeling annoyed. "I just can't believe they're doing this. They're trying to pin everything on a dead man. If they get away with this, that means that all of these plaintiffs will get nothing for their suffering. I know what you're saying – criminal acts have often been held by the courts to be a superseding cause of harm. If this court agrees with them, I guess we're just going to have to take it to a higher court. An appellate court. At any rate, I'm going to have to try to find a case on point for us. This is not how I wanted to spend my time preparing for this case."

"Well, welcome to the world of torts. Of personal injury cases. You have to understand one thing – you're going against deep pockets. These deep pockets are paid the big bucks to come up with all kinds of bullshit arguments designed to throw you off your game. They're paid to wear you down, bury you with paperwork and motions, so you just give up. I know, I was one of those corporate lawyer goons at one time. Sometimes, as here, the arguments are just plausible enough that you don't really know how to combat them. You know it's a bullshit argument. You can smell it from a mile away. But is it a winning argument for them? It might be. All that's known is that you're going to have to spend time, money, and attention, figuring it out."

The Trial

AND SO, for the next couple of weeks, that's what I did. I got knee-deep into legal research and wrote out a very carefully crafted answer to their motion to dismiss. All the while, there was a nagging voice inside my head telling me that there was something more to this whole thing than what met the eye. I just couldn't quite put my finger on it.

Finally, it was the day of the court hearing on the motion to dismiss. I was sitting there at the plaintiff's table, looking over at the defense table, and I immediately saw a team of five men sitting at that table. All of them were dressed in high dollars suits, their winged-tip shoes polished to an impeccable shine, so I could almost see my reflection in these shoes. They all had matching haircuts, almost matching ties, and they seemed to me to be undifferentiated, fungible. Like they were just one mass sitting at the defense table instead of individuals. I imagined their names were things like Tip and Biff and they all rowed crew at Harvard.

When I saw one of them sniff, I felt just a little bit vindicated. I didn't know if the guy had a cocaine problem, but he was sniffing like he did, and I took a kind of *schadenfreude* at the prospect. Other than him, however, I imagined I was facing the affluenza crowd. Men who never had to answer to anything, who got away with everything, and who just kept plugging along, oppressing people for a living.

Men who helped their drug company client get away with murder.

The judge called the case to order and then he called on me and the lead counsel for Columba. His name was Jack Meyer, and, like the rest of his undifferentiated, fungible, team, he was around 6 foot tall, with close-cropped hair, a navy blue tailored suit, a white shirt, and a red tie. He was generically handsome, with his dark hair and and big brown eyes, his lips bow-shaped and ruby red.

He smiled at me but I did not smile back. All that I could see was that he was trying to make sure his company did not have liability for making many children sick.

"Okay," Judge Warner, the judge assigned to this case, said. "We are here today on a motion to dismiss filed by counsel for the defendant, Jack Meyer. As I understand it, the defendant has claimed the criminal act taken by one Andrew Garvey was an act not foreseeable by the defendant, Columba Inc., a San Diego-based pharmaceutical company. Furthermore, the defendant has claimed the injury the plaintiff suffered was not a foreseeable one. Plaintiff has claimed the injury was foreseeable, because the inspection mechanisms at the Columba plant were not sufficient, therefore it was foreseeable that a contaminated inhaler might slip through the cracks. However, it's my understanding that discovery has not been exchanged between the parties, so the plaintiff does not know whether or not the inspection mechanisms of the Columba plant actually are insufficient. Therefore, the plaintiff has argued this motion is premature at any rate. Do I state the arguments of both parties correctly?" he asked.

"Yes, Your Honor," I said. "That's the dispute, in a nutshell."

He nodded. "I read through both the motion, and the response to the motion, and I'm leaning in a certain direction. I'm inclined to agree with the plaintiff that this motion is premature. Discovery has not gotten underway, as of yet, so the plaintiff has no idea if the defendant was negligent at all."

Jack cleared his throat. He was obviously ready for this

particular argument. "With all due respect, Your Honor, we understand that discovery has not really been commenced. Our office was trying to be respectful to the plaintiff because we understand her time is precious, so it would be pointless to ask to conduct discovery in this case if this court ruled the crime that was committed by one Andrew Garvey, the final layer inspector, superseded and broke the chain of causation. And that's what we contend. Case law is clear that intentional acts, such as those committed by Andrew Garvey, are not foreseeable. And as I had indicated in my motion to dismiss, it certainly was not foreseeable that children would be sickened by a disease so rare that nobody in the mainstream had even heard of it. A disease so rare that only 100 children, actually less than 100 children, have ever come down with it. That is not a foreseeable harm. So even if Columba was negligent in some way, and I am in no way stating that's true, but even if it were true, an unforeseeable act and an unforeseeable injury is superseding. Columba was not the proximate cause of these children's injuries. So, with all due respect, I do not know what is the relevance of whether or not Columba had lax inspection protocols. Again, I'm not saying Columba does have lax inspection protocols, I'm just stating that even if they did, that is not relevant to our case."

I took a deep breath. "I have to admit that that's a new one on me. Whether or not a company was negligent isn't relevant. I can't even believe he made that argument."

Judge Warner nodded. "I understand your argument, Mr. Meyer, but I don't agree with it. Let the discovery go forward and then maybe I will entertain a motion to dismiss if I find your company did not do anything wrong. Even if I do not dismiss the case, you could certainly make the argument to the jury that your company is not responsible for the injury to these children. You can see if the jury buys the argument. I, however, am not inclined to buy this argument. At least not yet. So, as I said, exchange discovery and I will put a time limit on when discovery has to be in. Then, at the end of your discovery, if there is still a basis for a motion to dismiss, I will listen to it. But not until then."

Jack looked annoyed. He clearly was not used to losing.

"Let's chat in the hallway," he said to me after the judge left the bench.

I followed him out into the hallway and the two of us took a seat on the bench right outside the door of the courtroom. "Listen, I am authorized to offer settlement to your client. Understand that we don't have to do this. Mr. Garvey was a criminal, plain and simple. Nobody could have foreseen that he would do what he did. But, bearing that in mind, I'm authorized to offer a settlement of $10,000 to your client."

I had to stop myself from laughing at him. "My client is a seven-year-old boy who has not been in school for over a year now. Not been in school because he's been enduring round after round after round of chemotherapy and radiation. His mother was convinced that she was going to have to bury him soon. She had his funeral clothes picked out for him. She doesn't have anything in her life except for this child, and I can tell you that the two of them have been going through hell. Not to mention the fact that my client's mother has been drowning in medical bills. Her insurance company has finally agreed to pay for experimental procedures to help save her child's life, but she still has a $15,000 deductible she has to pay not to mention thousands upon thousands in co-pays. Your $10,000 offer wouldn't even begin to scratch her medical bills, let alone the pain-and-suffering that both my client and my client's mother are going through. So you know what you can do with your $10,000 offer."

Jack shook his head. "You're rolling the dice. I'm going to show the jury that Mr. Garvey was a psychotic criminal and there was no indication when my client hired him that he was a psychotic criminal. There will be no negligent hiring case to be made here. When Mr. Garvey was hired, he was squeaky clean. He had not gotten so much as a parking ticket. Clean as a hound's tooth, as they say."

I had to laugh. "Well, if you're going to be throwing out old southern idioms, let me throw one out to you. That dog don't hunt. I'm not intimidated by you in your $500 haircut, your thousand dollar wingtip shoes, your tailored suit that goes with your tailored life that you're getting paid a thousand dollars an hour to create and pursue bullshit arguments like the ones you're making here. I think you're covering up. I don't know exactly what you're covering up, but it's something. And trust me on this when I tell you – I *will* figure it out. If it's the last thing I do, I'll figure it out."

He smiled a smarmy smile which was a combination of a smirk and a bigger smirk. "You're so sure I'm covering up for something?"

"Positive."

I just didn't know quite what it was.

Chapter Fourteen

IN THE MEANTIME, this case was absolutely blowing up in the media. It started with the New York *Times* story that covered the case of Frankie and how the insurance company agreed to cover his illness with the experimental procedure. I was in touch with Lorinda, and, while she was thrilled, over the moon, that Frankie was responding so well to treatment, she wasn't exactly comfortable with the attention she was getting in the news.

"I got reporter after reporter calling me and I don't know what to say. I just tell them about Frankie and about how great he's doing, but they seem to want something more from me. The only good thing is that there have been more people coming to the club to see me. I guess I'm kinda a celebrity these days."

With the media attention came the inevitable, though - panic. It turned out there were quite a few of those inhalers out in the world, and, in addition to the 20 children who had actually come down with mesothelioma, there were thousands more children who had come in contact with this

The Trial

inhaler. This inhaler had been marketed around the world, too, so there were scores of panicked parents whose kids weren't sick, but were bound to eventually get sick, sooner or later. Probably sooner, considering the amount of asbestos detected in the inhalers that had actually sickened the currently ill children.

After the panic came the conspiracy theories. Suddenly, there were stories popping up everywhere, all over social media, all over the web, that all inhalers were contaminated with asbestos. Not just the inhalers from Columba, not just the dry powder inhalers, but all inhalers from any company was suspect. This story had legs. All at once, it wasn't just parents whose children were using the Spiritus inhaler who were freaked out. Every parent with a child using an inhaler was terrified that their child had been exposed to asbestos. No matter where that inhaler came from, no matter who manufactured it, no matter if it was a dry powder or another kind of inhaler – the mist inhalers were also implicated - all inhalers were implicated, at least if you believed the conspiracy theorists on the web. Never mind the fact that it didn't make a lot of sense that an inhaler that uses mist would be able to transmit powdery asbestos. All the parents knew was that if their child was using an inhaler, their child was exposed.

Into the void came another pharmaceutical company, Tiberius Pharmaceuticals, that came out with a drug, Canbintrine, that promised to help these parents because it was marketed as a preventive measure to people who had been exposed to asbestos. It had been previously marketed to adults exposed to asbestos and it had obtained FDA approval the year before for childhood use. Prior to the panic, the drug had sold a few units to parents worried that their child had eaten contaminated crayons or worried their child's old school building might contain asbestos. But with the whole Columba scandal making the headlines, suddenly, pharmacies couldn't keep the drug on the shelf anymore. It seemed like every parent who had a kid with an inhaler, any inhaler, not just the inhalers made by Columba, was clamoring to get this particular drug for their kid.

The promise made to these parents was that if a child takes the drug on a regular basis for five years, the chances of the child ever being diagnosed with mesothelioma was greatly reduced. I had personally never heard of this drug before, even though it had been on the market for over a year. Suddenly, I couldn't turn on the television without seeing an ad for it. I saw cartoon ads for it, where a little cartoon version of a lung started out black and ended up pink and healthy as it followed around a young woman with red hair. Other ads were serious, with a very somber male voice intoning about "has your child been exposed to asbestos? With the recent controversy concerning a dry powder inhaler marketed by Columba Pharmaceuticals, many parents are feeling anxious and afraid. But there is hope. Canbintrine is the only preventive treatment for mesothelioma. If your child has been exposed to asbestos, ask your doctor if Canbintrine is right for you."

And, just like that, thousands of parents decided that Canbintrine was right for their kid.

Unfortunately, Canbintrine wasn't right for the parents with children who were already sick. Some of the kids apparently were getting the same treatment that Frankie got, immunotherapy, and they, too, were responding. Others were not so lucky, but it was certainly helpful that this case was getting so much attention in the news. No insurance company dared deny treatment to any of these kids, as they tried to deny Frankie for so long, which meant the kids were getting any and all treatment that might help them. Not just the standard chemo and radiation, but immunotherapy, gene therapy and epigenetic therapy.

However, not all the kids were as lucky as Frankie. Some of the kids, no matter what was tried, got sicker and sicker.

Finally, I read in the paper that one of the children, Meredith Bax, had died.

I felt my heart sink into my shoes when I read that. I looked up to the sky and cursed Andrew. "Are you happy now, you motherfucker?" I asked, shaking my fist impotently. "You took your first life. Her death is on your head. You won't be forgiven for this. You should burn in hell for this. Which you probably already are. You psychotic piece of shit."

I knew Meredith was only the beginning, which only enraged me more.

Then, on the day that Meredith was laid to rest, I got my first break in the case.

A man who identified himself only as X called me and gave me some information that stunned me.

And suddenly, I knew I was right.

There was much more to this case than I had ever realized.

Or could ever imagine.

Chapter Fifteen

May 18 – The Day Before Trial

I WAS GETTING ready for my first day of trial against Columba Pharmaceuticals. The company had made one ridiculous offer after another and I was sick of it. Their highest offer was only $50,000, which was laughable, considering how much damage they had done.

Frankie was now in remission and was able to attend the trial. It was a miracle that he had responded so well to the immunotherapy treatment. Just as I told Michelle Wilson, the Blue Cross/Blue Shield adjuster who went to bat for Frankie - she was crowing about that in the news incessantly, so much so that I was tired of hearing it - there was a Nobel Prize in the offing for the researchers who created the drug that helped Frankie. Because it wasn't just Frankie who went into remission through this new treatment, but 10 of the other kids who got sick, the researchers who created this immunotherapy treatment received the Nobel Prize for medicine.

The Trial

As for the makers of the drug Canbintrine, they clearly felt that they, too, were entitled to a Nobel Prize, but there would be no way to know if their drug was effective for several more years. So they were going to have to wait a little while longer.

I refused any and all settlement offers because I had knowledge that Columba didn't know I had. It wasn't like the information I got from the whistle-blower, whose identification I never did find out, was public information. In fact, it was very well-hidden. I exchanged my discovery with the lawyers for Columba, and they did the same, but they were not aware that I knew the piece of information they were desperately trying to keep secret.

And I had realized something else - Andrew Garvey was, most likely, a patsy. He was suicidal to begin with, which was something else I'd found out when I spoke with his widow, his estranged wife, Barbara. He had been suicidal ever since his daughter had died. His mental issues were well-known at his work, as he had apparently attempted suicide several times and all of his co-workers knew about it.

He was the perfect patsy for the real culprit in this case.

Christian was my second-chair and we were working 12-hour days getting ready for this case. I was getting more and more comfortable with Christian. I trusted him implicitly and I always knew he had my back.

Alexis, the domestic attorney down the hall, teased me about our closeness, but I never thought anything of it. "Boy, you guys sure do like working together," she said, stirring her coffee while she stood in my doorway. "What's going on with you two?"

I just shrugged. I didn't really like Alexis that much. She struck me as one of the mean girls that tormented me in high school. Tall, blonde, fit and impeccably dressed, yet exhibiting an aura of perpetual cool. She had a sometimes biting sense of humor, where she made fun of people behind their backs and then protested that she was "just kidding." My mother always taught me that behind every mean crack, there was usually truth there, no matter how much the person tried to claim they were kidding.

"We just work well together, I guess," I said. "And I won't lie. There's going to be a large judgment coming from this case. I think Christian is all-in because of that alone."

"You're so sure?" Alexis said, sitting down in my office, despite the fact that I didn't invite her to do so.

"Reasonably. I mean, anything can happen, as you well know. But I have some pretty good information in this case that I think will result in some pretty good punitive damages."

She cocked her head. "Punitives? I mean, I know the inhalers were tampered with deliberately, but it was a lone wolf who did it, and he's dead. Not to mention broke. I'm sorry, but I just don't see it. Christian told me you guys barely survived the last motion to dismiss."

That was a dicey scenario, I had to admit. I never told any of the attorneys about what I knew, because I wanted to keep it close to the vest. So I went into the hearing on the second motion to dismiss pretending I still believed that Andrew Garvey contaminated the inhalers. We already had exchanged our discovery and I admitted that I could find no evidence of negligence on the part of Columba.

It was touch and go, but the judge ended up allowing the case to go forward.

Jack Meyer wasn't pleased. "But Your Honor, counsel for the plaintiff just admitted that she could find no evidence of negligence on Columba's part. Columba could not foresee that its final inspector would sabotage those inhalers. It's an intentional act and Columba isn't responsible for it."

Judge Warner just shook his head. "I'll let the jury decide. I'm not comfortable dismissing this case just because so many children have been affected by this. I don't want to set a precedent like that, because if I do, the other children who have been sickened by these inhalers might also see their cases dismissed. I'll let the case go through for that reason alone."

That stumbling block cleared, it was full steam ahead.

"Ah, well, we got through it, didn't we?" I said to Alexis. "Listen, I don't have to tell you what we have up our sleeves. Suffice to say that we have something good that we're going to spring at them at just the right time."

She rolled her eyes. "I would have taken a settlement," she said in an imperious tone. "Just sayin'."

"Duly noted."

It all came down to this day.

Chapter Sixteen

May 19 – The First Day of Trial

I GOT to the courthouse with Christian, lugging a huge box of discovery behind me on a wheeled cart. When I arrived in the courtroom, I looked over at the gallery and saw that Frankie and Lorinda were already there. Frankie was smiling and wearing a Travis Kelce Kansas City Chiefs football jersey and jeans. I went over to them, and Lorinda gave me a hug.

"I'm sorry that Frankie is wearing that jersey," she said, pointing to him. "Travis Kelce came into the hospital and gave it to him and he signed it, too. I can't get Frankie to take it off. Travis is his hero."

I had to smile. Somehow, when I lived in Kansas City, we never fielded a decent team. But Patrick Mahomes and Travis Kelce had changed all that. Even I got into Kansas City football these days. After all, they were really my home team and San Diego presently had no team at all.

"Don't worry," I said. "Frankie probably won't testify

The Trial

today. I have too many other people lined up. I doubt you'll testify today, either."

She nodded. "Well, just tell me when you think we'll be testifying and I'll do my best to get him out of that thing. I need to wash it, anyway."

I went over to Frankie, seeing how much weight he had gained and how his skin was looking so much better. Before, he was pale and grey. He could barely open his eyes when I went to see him, aside from the first time I saw him, when he was having a particularly good day. But most of the times, when I saw him, he was in his bed and was barely able to turn his head to look at me.

Now, he had gained about 20 lbs back and was standing straight and tall, a huge smile on his handsome face. He came over to hug me, and I hugged him back, feeling his muscles and knowing the only reason why he was no longer skin and bone was because of a miracle.

He wasn't out of the woods. The doctors had not yet declared him cured. But they were no longer talking like his illness was incurable. They had proclaimed him to be in remission and cancer-free. But he still had to be constantly monitored. He had to see his doctor every week and would have to do so for several years.

But to hear Frankie tell it, his sickness was the best thing that ever happened to him. "I feel so great and I've met so many superstars. I would have never met all these famous people if I didn't get sick."

He would tell me, every time I saw him in the hospital, who had stopped by to say hello. "Demi Lovato came to see me today," he would tell me, his face beaming. "She's so pretty. Yesterday, it was Justin Bieber. I'm a Belieber now. And Taylor Swift came with Travis Kelce, of course. They're such a cute couple."

And so it went. Nick Jonas, Halsey, Cardi B, Adele, Miley Cyrus - just about every hot star had visited him. He always told me that he felt just like a star when they would come.

Still, I wanted justice for him. He was handling it all like a champ and he was home and doing well in school. But I knew he was scared that it would come back. His mother was terrified of the same thing.

I thirsted for justice for him. I also knew that if I could get a big settlement, that would be a great sign for all the other kids whose parents were also suing the company. The dominoes would start to fall, and if I could convince the jury to slap these bastards down, the company would no-doubt settle with all the other parties for similarly large amounts.

And then they would be broke.

They rolled the dice, hoping that Andrew Garvey's death would end it and they would get off scot-free.

They gambled and lost, as far as I was concerned.

Chapter Seventeen

OUR JURY WAS SELECTED, pre-trial motions were heard, and it was time to get down to brass tacks. I decided to waive my opening statement, just because I didn't want the company to know what I knew about them. I wanted the element of surprise to catch them off-guard.

Nevertheless, the other side decided to grandstand in their opening statement.

Because, of course.

"Ladies and gentlemen, this case..." Jack began. He shook his head, a smile on his face, as if he was trying to say that he just couldn't believe he was in front of them trying this case. What was I thinking, that I would make him try this case, when this case was clearly such a dead dog loser? That was the look on his face. "Let's just say the plaintiff has no case. Here are the facts. My client, Columba Pharmaceuticals, is an upstanding and up-and-coming pharmaceutical firm. As part of their portfolio, they manufacture asthma inhalers. One such inhaler, called Spiritus, was contaminated with asbestos. Now, I know what you're thinking.

You're thinking a dry powder inhaler manufactured by my client was tainted with asbestos, therefore my client was negligent, so open and shut. I know that you're sitting there thinking I'm wasting your time because I should've settled this case a long time ago on behalf of my client. But there's more to the story. Of course. Because if that's all the story was, you're right – this case would've gone away a long time ago.

But here's what really happened. My client, Columba Pharmaceuticals, hired a man by the name of Andrew Garvey. When my client hired this man named Andrew Garvey, there was no indication there was anything wrong with him. His background was clean as a whistle. You'll hear evidence that he had no criminal record, no psychiatric stays in his background, not even a parking ticket. What he did have was a scientific background, a PhD in chemistry to be exact, and he was very well-qualified. What he did was monstrous, however. His role at the company was to be an inspector for all the inhalers manufactured at the plant. He was the final inspector for the inhalers. My client hired three layers of inspectors for the inhalers. The first layer of inspector was the initial inspector, and if there was anything wrong with any one of inhalers, and the first layer of inspector found it, the inhaler would go back to the plant, and it was fixed. Then it would go back through the first layer of inspector, where it would go to the next layer. The second layer of inspector would check to make sure the problem found by the first layer was fixed. Andrew was the final layer of inspector. He was the final word for every one of the inhalers manufactured by this plant. He was the only one at this layer. In the first layer, there were 10 inspectors, all of them looking at inhalers. The second layer, there were five inspectors, all of them checking the work of the first

The Trial

layer. Once it all came down to Andrew, he signed off on every single one of the inhalers. Once these inhalers got through him, they were shipped out.

You'll hear evidence of the very tight security protocols my client has in place for these inhalers. In other words, there was not any negligence whatsoever. The other side will have a hard time trying to prove any kind of negligence. There was no products liability. In order to have a products liability case, you have to have negligence, and there was none.

What there was, was sabotage. A crime. This was a crime committed by Andrew Garvey. What he did, and he admitted to doing this in a deposition taken by opposing counsel, was sabotage the dry powder inhalers marketed towards children. These were inhalers decorated like little cartoon characters, or little elephants, or little clowns were painted on them. What he did was he took those inhalers and added asbestos into them. He explained that the reason why he did this was because his own daughter, Aurora, died of mesothelioma. That devastated him and he was frustrated because there was no treatment known to be effective for a child of that age who gets a disease that is so rare in children. He wanted there to be more research done on this disease in children and he realized that, since it was such a rare disease in children, there would never be any research done on it. He envisioned a day that a child might get sick with this disease and because he took actions he did, there would be a treatment plan for the child. So he decided to make children deliberately sick with this inhaler.

Mr. Garvey was a very sick and twisted individual, but my client had no way of knowing this was the case. He kept his twisted plan carefully hidden from everybody. Perhaps that's the reason he came to work for Columba, because he wanted to sabotage these inhalers. We may never know. What is known, however, is that he sabotaged them. But he was a lone wolf. That's important to know.

There is a doctrine in law called superseding causation. That doctrine pretty much says that if there was negligence with the company, which there was not here, but if there was negligence, and somebody does something intentionally to harm another person, this intentional act breaks the chain of causation for the harm done by the original tortfeasor. What that means is that even if Columba was negligent in some way, and as I stated before, this was not the case, but even if it were, the fact that Andrew harmed these children through an intentional act, a criminal act, would mean that my client, Columba, is not liable for any of the injuries. At any rate, there was not negligence, but there was an intentional act. There was only one person responsible for the harm done to these children, for the harm done to Frankie Jamison, and that person's name was Andrew Garvey. Unfortunately, Andrew Garvey is not available to be sued, as he is deceased. After he confessed all to counsel for the plaintiff, in a deposition, he went home and killed himself. Now the plaintiff could have sued his estate, but that would've gotten her nowhere, because he did not have an estate to speak of. He had no deep pockets.

My client does have deep pockets, therefore plaintiff targeted my client. But that's the only reason why the plaintiff has targeted my client. That's the only reason why the plaintiff did not go after Andrew Garvey, but went after Columba instead.

You will hear evidence that my client did nothing wrong. You will hear evidence that my client's security protocols are the strongest in the business. Nobody else has three layers of inspection for their inhalers. Only my client. To find negligence on the part of my client, you must find there is a duty, a breach of the duty, the breach of the duty caused the damages, and that there were damages. The plaintiff can show damages – there is no doubt that her client, Frankie Jamison, was a very sick boy. He was a very sick boy, but he is no longer, because he has been receiving treatment that has saved his life. That is to be applauded, of course. Everybody should rejoice in the fact that Frankie Jamison is getting better. But there is no doubt that he was sick and there is no doubt he was sick because he used an inhaler tainted 20% with asbestos powder. What the plaintiff cannot show is that my client breached any kind of duty to Frankie Jamison or anybody else.

Since the plaintiff cannot show a breach of a duty on the part of my client, then it's clear you must find for the defendant. Thank you very much for your time and attention and I know that after you hear the evidence, you will agree with me that the plaintiff does not have a case. This is a frivolous lawsuit and counsel for the plaintiff knows it."

At that, Jack sat down and smirked at me. I could see in his eyes that he thought he had me. He really believed I had no case and that I was just ready to flush the whole thing down the toilet.

He probably really thought that because I waived my right to an opening statement. If he was smart, he would've figured there was probably some strategic reason why I would waive my opening statement. But he obviously thought he was holding a winning hand and that I was just going through the motions.

He was going to find out differently.

And that was going to happen very soon.

Chapter Eighteen

AFTER JACK GAVE his opening statement, it was time for me to put on my case. The first person I decided to call was Dr. Ramirez. After Dr. Ramirez, I was going to call some of Frankie's doctors. By that time, it was probably going to be 5 o'clock, or probably even later. That was because most of the morning was taken up through jury selection and Jack's opening statement. I planned to call Frankie and Lorinda the next day.

Dr. Ramirez was sworn in, he stated his name, and I got right to business.

"Dr. Ramirez, can you please tell the jury what your specialty is?"

"I am an epidemiologist."

"As an epidemiologist, what do you exactly do?"

"I mainly work as a scientist and my job is to find the root causes of any kind of epidemics that might occur in certain populations. I study distributions and patterns of health and disease conditions in defined populations. I collect and analyze data and develop methodology used in clinical research, public health studies, and basic research."

"And, as an epidemiologist, is one of your duties outbreak investigation?"

"Yes."

"And what does that mean? What does it mean when you investigate an outbreak?"

"It means that when there is some kind of disease cluster, I investigate to find out what the commonalities are and what the causation is of the disease cluster. For instance, perhaps there is a population that has shown a certain kind of cancer cluster. Like, say, there's a certain cluster of glioblastomas, which is a very deadly brain cancer, within, say, a 5 mile radius of one another. This is an unusual outbreak of this kind of brain cancer, so I would investigate the environment around these individuals and try to pinpoint what the causation is of this particular outbreak. Or say there's an outbreak of salmonella at a school. It would be my job to find the causation of this outbreak of salmonella so I can pinpoint what changes the school needs to make to make sure it doesn't happen again."

"So, in your job, you often find environmental causes for disease clusters, right?"

"Yes. That is my job."

"And did you have an occasion to perform an outbreak study with children diagnosed with mesothelioma?"

"Yes. And the reason why I did the study was just because this was such an unusual disease. We're talking fewer than 100 children have been diagnosed with this disease ever in the history of medicine. Suddenly, I'm getting reports that five children have been diagnosed with it within the past year and then 20 children. When there's 20 children diagnosed with a disease within a short period of time, when there had been less than 100 children diagnosed with this disease ever, that is considered to be an outbreak."

"And when you found out all these children were being diagnosed with mesothelioma, what did you do?"

"I collected the data on the families of the children who have been diagnosed. I did a kind of ecological study that studied all the variables that were part of these children's lives, looking for a common variable."

"Did you find this common variable between all the children?"

"I did. I found, through my field examiners, that each one of these children was prescribed an inhaler called Spiritus. Spiritus was manufactured by Columba Pharmaceuticals. Since each one of these kids were prescribed the same inhaler, I had these inhalers tested."

"And what were the results of your testing?"

"Each one of these inhalers tested positive for asbestos. 20% asbestos. With this much asbestos being directly inhaled into the lungs of these kids, this was enough to cause mesothelioma in children genetically susceptible to the disease."

"Is it unusual?"

"Is it unusual for an inhaler to test positive for asbestos powder?"

"Yes. Is it unusual for inhaler to test positive for asbestos power?"

"Not just unusual. Unheard of. There has never been an inhaler that has ever tested positive for asbestos. I can say this definitively."

"So when you found out these inhalers did test positive for a high concentration of asbestos, what was your first conclusion?"

The Trial

"My only conclusion was that they were tampered with. Sabotaged."

"I have nothing further for this witness."

I sat down and Judge Warner addressed Jack. "Counselor, do you have any questions for this witness?"

Jack stood up. "No, Your Honor. In fact, I would like to stipulate that the Spiritus inhalers were the culprit in this disease cluster. I'm not going to dispute that, because, as I stated in my opening statement, I know these inhalers were the problem. So counselor for the plaintiff does not need to put on any other witnesses that will speak to how these kids got this disease."

Jack glared at me. He knew that I was going to be putting on witnesses that would make his company look bad. He wasn't having it. Not that I blamed him.

Nevertheless, I was going to have to pursue my case the way I wanted to.

So, for the next few hours, I called one doctor after another who treated Frankie. I wanted the jury to know how much he suffered. Frankie was going to testify himself the next day, along with Lorinda. It was important, for the issue of damages, that the jury knew how much pain and suffering was brought upon Frankie and Lorinda. Pain and suffering was going to be just one element of the damages I would have to show. I would also to have to show the issue of how much money Lorinda had to shell out on Frankie's behalf. That was very important.

It was important, but was not as important as showing exactly why this company should be punished to the fullest extent. Because what I found out from the whistleblower turned my stomach. I suddenly realized exactly what true evil was. True evil was a CEO worth billions of dollars, but that wasn't enough. A CEO who was such a sociopath that he didn't care who he hurt as long as he was getting his.

I was almost rubbing my hands together with glee, thinking about the days ahead, just thinking about the look on Jack's face when he realized how he had been played. The look on the CEO's face when I demonstrated to the world what kind of a monster he really was. I closed my eyes, imagining these looks, and I smiled to myself.

So, for the next few hours, one doctor after another talked about Frankie. About how Frankie started out as a sweet little six-year-old boy, with dark curls and big green eyes, who loved to play baseball and video games, and was already showing an interest in learning to play the guitar.

"His mother brought him in because she was concerned about him having shortness of breath," explained Dr. Baker, his pediatrician, who was the first one to see Frankie when he first got sick. "I knew he had a history of asthma so I was not concerned. However, his mother was concerned, because she told me his dry powder inhaler, the only inhaler that had ever helped him with his breathing issues, was no longer helping him. She told me that no matter how many times he used his inhaler, his shortness of breath just got worse."

"What kinds of tests did you order for Frankie?"

"I ordered a battery of tests. Of course, I didn't suspect for one second that he was suffering from mesothelioma, or even cancer that would have attacked his respiratory system, as these kinds of cancers are exceedingly rare in young children such as Frankie. I did order an imaging of Frankie's chest and found abnormalities, namely that there was a build-up of fluid around his heart. I then ordered the fluid be tested, and that's when Frankie was diagnosed with the disease."

The Trial

Then I called Frankie's oncologist, Dr. Washington, who explained to the jury the treatment plan Frankie went through. She described in detail the chemo and radiation treatments, and how Frankie lost his hair, lost 40 lbs and ended up getting down to only 80 lbs, and how he just got sicker and sicker. "Finally, I discussed hospice options with his mother, Lorinda," Dr. Washington said. "Because Frankie's insurance company was refusing to cover him for other treatments, I honestly believed that Frankie was end-stage."

I looked over at the jury and found they were all watching Dr. Washington with interest. Some of the women had tears in their eyes. I knew that many of the women had young children at home, around Frankie's age, and I could imagine they all were putting themselves into Lorinda's shoes. What if my child was diagnosed with this disease? was what they were all probably thinking.

As powerful as Dr. Baker and Dr. Washington's testimonies were, however, I knew their testimonies wouldn't be the nail in the coffin. Their testimonies would help the jury determine damages, however, especially pain and suffering and punitive damages, so I was very careful to elicit testimony that showed exactly how much Frankie suffered. Frankie's testimony, scheduled for the next day, would also connect the dots.

Then, after the jury was saturated with details of how much both Frankie and Lorinda suffered, I was going to perform the *piece de resistance*. The CEO for Columba, whose name was William Lanza , was on my witness list. As far as Jack knew, I had him on my witness list because I wanted to ask him, in detail, about the procedures the company used to ensure that no inhalers left the factory floor contaminated. I was sure that William was eager to tell the jury just how secure his factory was. He was going to expound on how the company just couldn't foresee that a lone wolf would do what he did.

Little did he know that I didn't really care to ask him any questions about safety procedures. No, I had him on my witness list for a much different reason.

And he would soon find out just what that reason really was.

Chapter Nineteen

May 20 – The Second Day of Trial

FRANKIE AND LORINDA testified the next day and their testimonies took the entire day. Jack chose to cross-examine neither Frankie nor Lorinda, figuring it wouldn't do any good, because his theory of the case was that his company wasn't liable to Frankie at all. Therefore, it was irrelevant, in Jack's view, about Frankie and Lorinda's damages. So he let their testimony slide without pushing back.

I pressed them about all they went through. Frankie told the court about how he couldn't eat for days, and how, when he tried to eat, he would just throw everything up. He told the jury about how he was convinced he was going to die and didn't want to bring that up to his mother because he didn't want to see her sad.

"I couldn't tell her that I knew I would go to heaven soon," he said to the jury and I saw there wasn't a dry eye in the house as he spoke. "I wanted to talk to her. I wanted her to know that I would be okay, because I learned in church that kids like me, we go to a better place. We go to a place where there's no more pain, no more needles, no more doctors. But I worried about her. I didn't think she would be okay."

"So you and your mom just didn't discuss it?"

"No. But I did try to say things that might make her happy after I died. Like I tried to get her to get a dog. She loves dogs. I knew a dog could never take my place, but I thought it might make her a little bit happy. I also tried to talk to her about finding a guy and having another kid. I wanted her to have something in her life after me, because I was scared that she would just not want to live if she lost me."

Kids were perceptive, that was for sure.

Lorinda, for her part, said much the same thing. "I couldn't talk to him about dying. I just couldn't. I wanted to. I knew it was the right thing to talk to him. But every time I tried, I would open my mouth and nothing would come out. I would just have to leave the room so Frankie could never see me crying."

Both Frankie and Lorinda told the jury about their constant fear about the next scan.

"What if I go to the doctor and find my cancer has come back?" Frankie mused out loud. "I'm so scared about that, every single day. Right now, I feel good. I'm back in school and I'll be playing Pee Wee baseball this summer. Second base. But it could all go away anytime and I think about that all the time."

As for Lorinda, she talked about her terror as well. "I take Frankie to the doctor each and every week. So far, his scans show he's cancer-free. He's in remission. But the doctors are always telling me that they have to monitor him closely because he could come out of remission at any time.

The Trial

And they've warned me that if the cancer comes back, it will be harder to treat next time. They've told me a recurrence would probably be something Frankie won't survive. They're doing all they can and they've told me that if Frankie can just live for another 4 1/2 years in remission, he might be able to grow up and live a full life. They've also reassured me they're developing new treatments every day so if Frankie can live out the next 4 1/2 years, he might be considered cured. Right now, the doctor says Frankie will never be cured. But that might change at any time."

I was carefully laying the groundwork for what was to come. I could see that Frankie and Lorinda had captured the jury, so I knew the award to come would be significant.

I just had to snare one unsuspecting person in my trap.

The second day of trial had come and gone and I went home to relax.

My next witness would be crucial and I had to be fresh as a daisy.

I had to be on my game so I could throw him off of his.

Chapter Twenty

May 21 – The Third Day of Trial

ON THE THIRD day of trial, it was time for me to call my witness. "The plaintiffs call William Lanza," I said.

I looked over at Jack's face and I could see his familiar smirk. He probably spent days, weeks, preparing this bastard for just how to lie to the jury about his company's culpability. I would imagine that was the case, anyhow.

I wasn't sure.

But I was sure of one thing - Jack was actively involved in a cover-up. I had actively sought certain documents, specifically asked for them, and Jack had always replied on his answers to my discovery requests that these documents did not exist.

I found out from the whistle-blower that they did. And I had them in my hot little hands.

William took the stand. He was a 50ish guy, dressed impeccably in a tailored suit, a little handkerchief in his pocket. He wasn't a bad-looking guy, as he was tall and fit, with salt-and-pepper hair, a straight aquiline nose and a square jawline. His brown eyes imitated a soulfulness the man himself did not possess. He walked straight and tall towards the witness stand and looked at me with an imperious expression, a similar expression to that of his corrupt minion, Jack Meyer. He even had a similar smirk on his face as I approached him.

I smiled as I envisioned that smirk being wiped right off.

"Mr. Lanza," I said, approaching him. I cocked my head a little to the left. "Do you understand why I called you to the witness stand today?"

"Of course," he said, glancing at Jack. "You wanted me to testify about the security protocols at my company, which I can assure you are second to none. But I will admit that I do not understand exactly why I'm here, because my company wasn't negligent. I could never foresee that a psychotic individual like Andrew Garvey would infect my company."

At that, he looked right at Frankie. "I'm very sorry, young Frankie Jamison, that you were sickened by your inhaler. Please know that if I had known that these inhalers were contaminated with asbestos, I would have moved heaven and earth to make sure that each and every one of them were recalled by my factory. But I didn't know. I couldn't know, because my last line of defense was the person who actually did the contamination. But I would do anything, young Frankie, to take away your pain."

I looked at his face and wondered what kind of game he was trying to pull. No, I knew what game he was playing. The victim card. The *I did nothing wrong, and I took my valuable time out to be here, but I thought it was important to come so that I can look at Frankie and express my sorrow* game. He was playing to the jury, making them see how put upon he was.

Poor, poor William.

I pressed on. "Mr. Lanza, I would like to ask you what relationship you had with one Andrew Garvey before you hired him?"

He smirked. "No relationship at all."

I looked over at the judge. "Permission to treat this witness as hostile," I said. I looked over at Jack's face and he looked perplexed. It was obvious he had no idea what was about to happen.

"Any objections?" Judge Warner asked Jack.

"None, your honor," Jack said.

"Very well. Ms. Collins, you may proceed."

"Thank you, Your Honor. Now, Mr. Lanza, I would like you to take a look at an email written by you to Mr. Garvey," I began.

At that, Jack was immediately on his feet. "Objection." And then he motioned to the judge. "May I approach?"

At that, the judge motioned both of us to come up to the bench. "Counselor, what is it that you needed to say to me?" he asked Jack.

"I don't think this email is admissible. I would like to have a meeting in chambers so we can go over this. Since Ms. Collins decided to blindside my client with this email, I think we need to seriously decide if it's going to be admissible, even if she can lay a foundation for it, which is doubtful."

I knew he was going to ask this and he was playing right into my hands. "I agree. We should take a short recess and talk about this in chambers."

The judge just nodded. And then he banged his gavel. "Ladies and gentlemen of the jury, the counsel for the defense has asked for a short recess to determine the admissibility of certain documents. So I would like to ask for a

The Trial

recess of 20 minutes. Please be back and ready to listen to some more testimony by 9:20 AM. Thank you very much."

The men and women of the jury filed out and Judge Warner led the way to his chambers. We got back there and I took a seat in front of Judge Warner's desk, while Jack took the other seat. I could practically see smoke coming out of his ears. If he was a cartoon character, that's what would be happening – both of his ears would be billowing out large clouds of gray smoke.

"Okay, counselor, what is your beef?" Judge Warner asked.

Jack pointed right at me. "She got that email illegally. I don't know how she got a hold of it, but she's not supposed to be in possession of it. Therefore, it is the fruit of the poisonous tree and it needs to be deemed inadmissible. We had a motion *in limine*, right before this trial was started, and she could've brought in that email in then. I'm sure that if she would've done that, Your Honor, with all due respect, you would've told her not to even go there."

Judge Warner looked right at me. "Well, counselor, is what Mr. Meyer is saying true?"

"It is true that I was not supplied this email by Mr. Meyer or his client. I will say that I have one other email in my possession that was written from Andrew Garvey to Mr. Lanza. I didn't get them from Mr. Meyer or his client, though. I got these emails from an individual who is anonymous, even to me. But this person obviously had access to these emails and this person printed them out and sent them to me."

Jack started pointing at me again. "You see? You see? She just admitted she got them not through the proper channels. Open and shut case of inadmissibility." At that, he leaned back in his chair, his arms crossed in front of him.

He was glaring at me, a glare that could have burned a hole right through my skin.

I just shook my head. "Listen, Your Honor, the only reason why I did not get these emails from Mr. Meyer, or his client, is because they chose not to give them to me. I have in my possession my request for production of documents that I sent to Mr. Meyer, along with some interrogatories that address this issue. As you can see, I specifically requested any and all communication between Mr. Lanza and Mr. Garvey. As you can see, on the interrogatories, Mr. Garvey marked those questions when I asked about the communication, N/A. Not applicable. You can also see that in my request for production of documents, when I asked for any and all communication between the two men, it was marked N/A. Now, as you can see, there were emails between the two men. One of these emails dates back to before Mr. Garvey even joined the company. These emails relate to exactly the reason why Mr. Garvey was hired, why Mr. Garvey confessed to tampering with the inhalers, and why he committed suicide. I do not know why a savvy person such as Mr. Lanza would put all of this into writing, except for that he probably thought he could get away with it. He never imagined that I, or any other attorney, would ever get a hold of these emails. I think it's pretty rich that counsel, Mr. Meyer, would scream about my getting these emails illicitly, when the only reason why I had to get them illicitly is because he was covering up their existence in the first place."

It was my turn to cross my arms in front of me and glare. Then I leaned back and smirked right at Jack. While I did that, Jack was not looking at me, which told me everything I needed to know.

There was a question in my mind as to whether or not

The Trial

Jack knew about the existence of these emails. Maybe when he asked the sleazoid William Lanza about it, William just told him these emails didn't exist. However, in noticing how he was not looking at me, I think he knew all along. I think he knew he was suppressing evidence from me while covering up for his boss.

"Well," Judge Warner finally said, looking right at Jack. "I can clearly see that Ms. Collins asked for communication between Mr. Garvey and Mr. Lanza, repeatedly, in her interrogatories and her requests for production of documents. Now you're telling me the only reason she has these emails is because she got them from somebody else? Is that what you're saying? You did not supply them to Ms. Collins pursuant to a proper discovery request? Actually, it's pursuant to several proper discovery requests."

He was caught and he knew it. "The reason why I did not give them to her is because I don't feel that she's entitled to them. They do not concern any kind of relevant matter in this case."

"First of all," I said. "You're grasping at straws when you say they do not concern a relevant matter in this case. Your company is trying to pin everything on this one man, Andrew Garvey. These emails show what the real situation is regarding Mr. Garvey. These emails go to the very crux of this case. So as for your relevancy argument, I think the judge would agree that's not a good argument. And secondly, even if you did deem them not to be relevant, just not supplying them and covering them up is not the proper way of refusing them. I can't believe I have to tell you procedure 101, but it looks like I have to. You do not just ignore my requests. You apply for a protective order and let the judge decide if the emails are relevant or not. You didn't do that. You just ignored my requests for them. You just lied on your responses to my discovery requests. You said they didn't exist. I'm sorry, but you don't get to decide on your own whether or not I get documents I asked for."

I looked over at the judge, who was glaring at Jack. *Checkmate.*

The judge just shook his head. "I can't even believe you're sitting here in my chambers, Mr. Meyer, trying to make the argument that the reason why you did not give these emails to Ms. Collins is because you, yourself, deemed them not to be relevant. I don't have to tell you that Ms. Collins is absolutely right. If you don't want to give up something opposing counsel is asking for, then it's up to you to file a motion to quash the request and seek a protective order. You didn't do any of that. You just decided on your own that you were not going to give her these documents, and, as she noted, you lied about it. I'm inclined to hold you in contempt of this court. At any rate, as long as she can lay the foundation with your client, and hopefully he's not going to lie about it and say he had nothing to do with these emails, she can certainly admit these emails into evidence."

Jack's face was very pale. "I'm very sorry, Your Honor."

"As I said before, I'm inclined to hold you in contempt," Judge Warner said. "I'll decide about that after I hear what your client has to say on the stand. As I said, I can tell by the way you're acting that you knew these emails existed. You knew they existed, you knew they were a problem, and that's why you said they did not exist on your discovery responses. Which means your client better do the right thing and own up to them. If he doesn't, I will hold both of you in contempt. And that is my ruling."

Jack just nodded. "When I get back into the courtroom, can I ask for some extra time to confer with my client?"

"Yes. Because you're going to have the tell him what's

The Trial

what here. You're going to have to tell him that if he lies on the stand, I will find out about it. I will dig and dig and dig until I find out the truth. And then I will report him for perjury to law enforcement. You need to tell him the penalty for perjury is 4 years in prison and that committing perjury is a felony. In other words, you better tell him to tell the truth."

"And, Your Honor, I have in my possession a copy of some agreements Mr. Lanza made with Mr. Garvey," I said. "It was the same deal - I got these agreements through an anonymous source because Mr. Meyer lied on his discovery requests and said there were no such agreements. I would like a ruling on those, as well."

At that, I gave Judge Warner a copy of the agreements I had.

"This will also be admissible for the same reason, Mr. Meyer. And, as I said before, your client better own up to these agreements, or, I swear to God, I will throw him in jail."

Jack, clearly chastened, just nodded.

The judge led us back out into the courtroom and Jack immediately went over to William Lanza and motioned for him to go into the conference room just outside the courtroom doors.

I looked over at Frankie and Lorinda. "What's going on?" Lorinda asked me in a low voice.

"I don't really know. What I do know is that the judge is pissed. He's going to be ready to send everyone to jail by the time this is over with. Let's just say they tried to get away with something they should not have tried to get away with."

Not 10 minutes later, Jack came back into the courtroom with William. Jack was glaring at me. But his glare was nothing compared to what William was doing. He was caught. That was all there was to it. Both of them were squirming like two fishes on a hook.

Jack motioned to me. "Why don't we go into the conference room and we can talk settlement."

I shook my head. "The time for that has come and gone. No way am I going to enter into a confidential settlement, which means the public will not know what your CEO did and why he did it. You see these reporters in this courtroom?" I asked, pointing at several of the reporters hanging around in the gallery, their microphones at the ready. "I want them to get the story. I know you want this whole thing to go away. At this moment, you would like nothing more than to sweep it all under the rug. Buy our silence. But I'm here to tell you, that ain't happening. So you can try to talk settlement all you want, but nobody's listening."

I looked over at Lorinda and she nodded. She obviously agreed with every word I said.

Jack bit his lower lip. If I had any doubt that Jack did not know about the existence of these emails, all that doubt had been erased. Just the fact that he only took a few minutes to confer with his client, before busting out a settlement offer, meant the two men had obviously talked about this very scenario before court ever began. I could just imagine them, in the bunker, hashing out Plan B, which was what would happen in the event I actually got my hands on the emails they sought to hide. No, if Jack didn't know about the emails beforehand, his conversation with William would have been much, much longer.

"Okay then, I guess let's just continue on."

"Looks like you're not going to be asking to have the case dismissed anymore."

The Trial

He said nothing to that. He just gave me a dirty look.

The jury came back again, the judge called the case to order, and William took the witness stand once more. "I would like to remind the witness that he is still under oath," Judge Warner said. "And I would like to remind the witness that he is being treated as hostile. Which means that Ms. Collins, counsel for the plaintiff, may ask you leading questions. Ms. Collins, you may proceed."

I nodded. "I would like to show you what has been marked as plaintiff's Exhibit A. Can you please identify this document for the jury?"

He studied it as if he had never seen it before. Then he handed it back to me, a look of disgust on his face. "It's an email between myself and Mr. Andrew Garvey."

"So, is it your testimony that you are the author of this particular email?"

"I am."

"And this email was sent from your private server to Mr. Garvey, isn't that right?"

"Yes. That's right."

"And the content of this email is a true representation of your actual words, right?"

"What do you mean?"

"I mean, did you write this email? Are these your words?"

"Yes. I said I did."

"Good. Now, I would like for you to read the contents of this email to the jury."

At that, he glared at Jack, his eyes telling him he would be fired. Typical. He was probably the kind of guy who would blame everybody but himself for the shenanigans he caused. He put on a pair of glasses and proceeded to read the email.

"Dear Mr. Garvey. You don't know me, but I read about your case in the paper. I would like to extend my condolences to you for the loss of your precious daughter, Aurora. I understand that she passed away of an extremely rare form of childhood cancer, mesothelioma. That's a devastating diagnosis. I understand, from the newspaper article I read, that you are currently looking for work. I would like to extend an invitation for you to interview for a position at my company, Columba Pharmaceuticals. I understand from the article that you have a PhD in chemistry and I believe you would be a good fit for our company. I'm looking forward to hearing from you. I think you'll find some of the advances our company is looking into are very exciting indeed."

"So, Mr. Lanza," I said. "Would you like to answer my earlier question a little bit differently, and that question was, what relationship did you have with Mr. Garvey before he interviewed with your company?"

He knew this particular email seemed innocent enough but he also had to know what was coming. He was going to have to calculate exactly how to answer this question, and how innocent he would act. He knew the jig was up, at any rate. There was no point in trying to hide anymore.

"Okay, so I headhunted him. No different from any other individual I headhunt."

"So there's not a qualitative difference between you writing a man you read about in the paper who lost his daughter to a very rare disease and asking him to apply for a prominent position in your company, and headhunting. Is that what you're saying?"

"That's exactly what I'm saying."

"But isn't it true the only reason why you were headhunting this particular person is because his daughter died of a rare form of cancer?"

The Trial

"I felt badly for him, that's all. I cannot imagine losing a child. His daughter was only seven years old. The same age as your client, Frankie Jamison. I took pity on him and I offered him a job."

Oh. So he was going to play this game. The innocent game. Despite him knowing what was coming down the pike.

Well, that's on him.

That's on him.

"Isn't it true, Mr. Lanza, that prior to hiring Mr. Garvey, you looked into his background? You talked to some of his friends, or you had a private investigator talk to some of his friends. And you found out that he had attempted suicide twice since his daughter died, isn't that right?"

For good measure, I had the friends who he had spoken with lined up to testify about exactly what was going on.

William looked at me, obviously calculating as to whether or not he wanted to lie about this. He looked over at the jury and I could practically see him spinning in his head. "Yes," he finally said. "That's another reason why I wanted him to apply for this job. I didn't know him. I only knew what I read about him in the paper, so I did hire some private investigators to find out more about him before I asked him to apply. When I found out he had attempted suicide twice, I knew I had to give him a reason for living. I'm very empathetic that way."

I practically snorted. "Very empathetic." *More like pathetic.* "Now, Mr. Lanza, I would like you to read aloud what I have marked as Exhibit B. Can you identify this document?"

He read it, his face getting paler and paler. "It's an email that Andrew Garvey sent to me."

"So you are the recipient of this email, correct?"

"Yes, I was the recipient of this email."

I had to smile. This was the email, the kind of email, that I was sure he had wiped clean off of his server. He probably thought he would never have to answer for this. Yet, here he was, doing just that.

Jack was on his feet. "I would like to object to the hearsay."

"Your Honor, Mr. Lanza has confirmed that he was the recipient of this email. And, at any rate, this email does not go to the truth of the matter asserted, so it's not hearsay."

Jack finally took a deep breath. "I think we're going to have to have another meeting in chambers, because we need to go through each one of these emails and determine if they are relevant and if they are hearsay. I will stipulate the emails that my client sent to Andrew Garvey are not hearsay, provided he identifies them as his own words. But any email from Mr. Garvey written to my client could possibly contain hearsay, or be hearsay. I think we need to hash this out."

The judge tapped his fingers on the bench, considering what Jack was saying. "Here's what I'm going to do. I will take these emails, on a case-by-case basis, and I will read them through before they are presented to the witness. And then I will make my ruling as to whether or not they are hearsay. So I would like to see Exhibit B, Ms. Collins, and hopefully you can explain to me why you believe it is not hearsay."

He read the email and then he looked at me.

"Your Honor, I'm not offering this email as the truth of what is being asserted in the email. I'm simply offering the email to go to Mr. Garvey's state of mind."

"So, you're not going to offer this email as proof of an agreement between Mr. Garvey and Mr. Lanza?"

The Trial

While the judge was reading the email, Jack was doing the same. "I don't agree, Your Honor. This email does not fall under the state of mind exception and I don't see how it could possibly be proffered for anything but showing an alleged agreement between Mr. Garvey and Mr. Lanza."

I knew I would have a hard time getting this particular email in, which was fine. I had other emails that could prove my case, but this was one of the most damning.

The judge appeared to think about what I was saying. "I will allow it. Please proceed."

I nodded. "Now, Mr. Lanza, can you please state for the record the date on this email."

"Yes. The date of this is October 29 of last year."

"October 29 of last year. I would like to enter into evidence a transcript of the deposition of Andrew Garvey taken on November 1 of last year, just two days after this email. I have highlighted the relevant portions for the jury to peruse. As this was a statement taken under oath, it is not hearsay."

I gave the judge and Jack a copy of the transcripts and then went over to the jury and passed around the portions where Andrew "confessed" to contaminating the inhalers because he wanted there to be more research done on childhood mesothelioma.

"Now," I said, turning my attention to William once more. "This email you received from Andrew was only 2 days before he confessed everything to me during the course of his deposition. He was found dead later on that same day. Do you dispute that he confessed everything in his deposition and committed suicide right afterwards?"

"No, why would I dispute that?"

"Okay," I said. "Could you please read the email dated

October 29 of last year, which is an email from Andrew Garvey to you?"

William looked at Jack expectantly, as if he was looking to him to stop this entire proceeding. Jack just looked helplessly on. The judge had already deemed this email admissible.

He cleared his throat. "William, as we discussed, I will commit suicide tomorrow after my deposition." He cocked his head. "And that's it. What does that prove?"

"What does that prove? It proves that you and he had an agreement he was going to commit suicide."

"It proves no such thing."

"Okay, what action did you take when you received this email? Did you go over to his house and try to talk him out of it? Did you send him an email back, trying to encourage him to seek help?"

"No. I'm a very busy man. Not to sound cold, but I don't have time for such things."

"No, you would not try to help him, because, after all, you and he had discussed him committing suicide beforehand."

He sighed. "I guess I should've done more about it. Looking back, I guess I should've tried to encourage him to seek help. That's on me."

"Now isn't it true you had an agreement with Andrew that, after he died, you would donate $1 million to the childhood oncology wing of the University of California San Diego Medical Center, with the understanding that this wing would be called the Aurora Garvey wing?"

"Yes, we had that agreement."

"In fact, you reduced this agreement to writing, didn't you?"

"Yes. We did."

The Trial

I handed him a copy of the agreement he had with Andrew. It was a standard contract, signed by both parties. "In fact, this contract that I have marked as Exhibit C is this reduction to writing of the agreement that you had with Mr. Garvey, isn't that right?"

I was connecting the dots, methodically. I was quite sure the jury had no idea where I was going with this. At the moment, it all seemed innocent enough. Granted, the email was pretty damning – to read between the lines, it was clear the two men had an understanding that Andrew was going to commit suicide. But I also knew the jury had no idea exactly *why* he was going to commit suicide or why Mr. Lanza would want him to.

"Yes," he said, looking at the contract. "This is an agreement we had that I would donate money in his daughter's name to the childhood oncology wing at the UCSD."

"Okay. So, here's what we know, just from this email, and this contract. We know that you and he had an understanding that he was going to commit suicide after his deposition, and we know you had agreed to donate $1 million to the UCSD childhood oncology wing in his daughter's name. Can you tell the court why you and he made that agreement?"

"I knew how passionately he felt about childhood cancer and I knew how proud he would be if there was a childhood cancer wing in a hospital named after his daughter."

"And that's it? Are you telling the court that's the only reason why you would have donated $1 million in Aurora Garvey's name after his death?"

I knew how suspicious it all looked. And I couldn't wait to tie all the dots together.

"Yes. That's it."

"Hmmm. Were you and Mr. Garvey particularly close?"

"I don't understand the question?"

"I mean, were you and Mr. Garvey actually close friends or was he just another employee to you?"

"He was special and I felt for him."

"But he was not a close friend?"

"No."

"So he really was just an employee to you?"

"I felt for him. And that's it."

"So you said. Did you happen to make any another other agreements with any of your other employees where you promised to donate a large amount of money in their name after their death, or was this an agreement you had just with Mr. Garvey?"

He swallowed hard. "Just with Mr. Garvey."

"There were other employees of Columba Pharmaceuticals that had gone through personal tragedies. In fact, there were at least three other employees who also lost children to childhood cancer. Isn't that right?"

"Yes, I suppose that's correct. It's not unusual for a parent to lose a child to that dread disease."

"Yet you didn't make any other agreement with anybody else who had lost a child through cancer while promising them that you would donate a large amount of money to a hospital in their child's name after the employee's death. Only Andrew Garvey, isn't that right?"

"Yes, obviously I can't be charitable with all my employees like that. But I decided that I to choose just one person who I was going to do to do that for and Andrew was the lucky one."

"He was the lucky one. And you knew he was going to kill himself. In fact, isn't it true that was the understanding you had with him? He would confess to contaminating those inhalers and then commit suicide so he could not be

The Trial

dragged into court because he might tell the truth. And in exchange for him doing that, you told him you would not only donate $1 million to the child oncology wing of the University of California San Diego in his daughter's name, but you would also give $1 million to his estranged widow, Barbara Garvey. Isn't that true?"

By now, he was squirming. "No, I did not have an understanding with him like that."

"But you did give $1 million to Barbara Garvey, didn't you?"

"I did."

"In fact, you reduced that particular agreement to writing before Andrew Garvey died as well, didn't you? You had a separate contract with Andrew Garvey that you would donate $1 million to Barbara Garvey after his death. And this is the contract, isn't it?"

He was breathing heavily. "Yes, that is a contract I made with him."

"I would like to enter the contract between Andrew Garvey and William Lanza, concerning Mr. Lanza's agreement to give $1 million to Barbara Garvey after Mr. Garvey's death, as Exhibit D."

I gave the judge a copy, Jack a copy, and I passed around a copy to the jury.

"Any objections?"

"No, Your Honor," Jack said.

"It is so entered. Please proceed," Judge Warner said.

"Now, I would like to enter into evidence the suicide note of one Andrew Garvey." I looked over at Jack, fully prepared to counter his inevitable objection that it was hearsay.

"Objection, hearsay," Jack said, getting to his feet.

"Dying Declaration, Your Honor. It was made by Mr.

Garvey who is not available, while he believed his death was imminent, and the suicide note concerns the circumstances of his death. Therefore, the suicide note meets all the criteria for the dying declaration exception to the hearsay rule."

I handed the suicide note to the judge, he looked it over, and handed it back. "I will allow it. Please proceed."

"Yes. Will you please read the highlighted portions to the jury?" I asked William.

"I, Andrew Garvey, am of sound mind and body. I am doing this for the good of all. I have been such a screwup my entire life, and this is the only good thing that I have done. Please know that I am very sorry for what I did. And I'm very sorry for taking this final act. I can only take this final act with a clear conscience, knowing that nobody's life will be negatively affected by my taking my own. In fact, lots of people will actually benefit from it, including my lovely wife, Barbara, and kids with cancer," William read to the jury.

"Okay. So, according to this dying declaration, this suicide note, Andrew was explicitly saying that lots of people were going to benefit from his dying. Isn't that right?"

"Yes. Obviously he was thinking that, because of the agreement I had with him."

Time to move in for the kill. "Isn't it true the only reason you hired this guy was because you were looking for somebody who could take the fall for contaminating those inhalers, because you contaminated these inhalers yourself?" I asked.

"Why would I do something like that?"

I ignored him. "And then you hired Mr. Garvey, because he was suicidal, and also because his daughter died of the very disease that you were going to try to disseminate to children all over the world. Isn't that right?"

"Of course not. Why would I do something like that?"

"And then you made an agreement with Mr. Garvey that he confess everything to me in a deposition, after which he would commit suicide, therefore not be available for any questions. Isn't that right?"

"You don't answer my questions. Why would I do something like that?"

"And the way you induced him to take the fall for you is through telling him you were going to donate money to his beloved wife, his estranged beloved wife, and, the kicker, that you would donate $1 million to combat childhood cancer, while enshrining his daughter's name into posterity. Isn't that true?"

He just shook his head. "I don't know what you're talking about."

"Mr. Lanza, are you associated with a company by the name of Tiberius Pharmaceuticals?"

"No."

"You're not? Did you not form a shell company by the name of Aesop Limited?"

I knew I had him. He thought he had formed the shell company anonymously, because he obviously did not want anybody to know he was behind this particular company. It took quite a lot of digging, and more than a little bit of arm-twisting, to find out he was behind this company. A bribe or two might have been made along the way, but I didn't want to get into that.

"Yes, Aesop Limited is my company."

"Oh. Well, isn't it true that Aesop Limited is actually the parent company of Tiberius Pharmaceuticals? In fact, isn't it true that Aesop Limited owns 100% of Tiberius Pharmaceuticals?"

"Yes," he said, clearly gritting his teeth. "Yes, Aesop Limited is the owner of Tiberius Pharmaceuticals."

"Yet you formed this Aesop Limited anonymously, didn't you?"

"Yes, I did, and I don't know how you found out about it."

"I have my ways. Anyhow, why did you form this company anonymously?"

He took a deep breath. "That's not your business."

"And isn't it true that Tiberius Pharmaceuticals has been manufacturing a drug called Canbintrine for years, marketed for adults?"

"Yes. That is Tiberius' marquee drug."

"What is Canbintrine?"

"It's a drug that, when taken on a consistent basis for five years, has been shown to prevent the manifestation of mesothelioma in individuals who have been exposed to asbestos."

"And the company has recently gotten FDA to approve a different version of Canbintrine, one targeted exclusively for children?"

"Right."

"Isn't it true that you formed Aesop Limited anonymously, because you didn't want anybody to know that you were involved in marketing this Canbintrine for children? You knew your company would be implicated in sickening children around the world with mesothelioma, and it wouldn't look good for anybody to know you were involved in marketing a drug manufactured with the express purpose of preventing mesothelioma from manifesting in children exposed to your inhalers. You knew how that would look, didn't you?"

And, I just tied it all together.

"No, that's not right. Listen, I have lots of corporations I'm involved with. Tiberius Pharmaceuticals is just one of them."

"How convenient. Your company caused a worldwide panic in parents buying inhalers for their children with asthma. Predictably, the media tried to make it clear that only your Spiritus dry inhalers were being recalled for asbestos contamination, but parents everywhere, no matter what kind of inhaler their child was using, no matter who manufactured it, panicked. It was predictable that the conspiracy theories would get going on social media, where posters everywhere were falsely stating that all inhalers, from every company, were being similarly contaminated with asbestos. Because of that, and because the Canbintrine for children drug was being marketed as the only drug that could prevent the manifestation of mesothelioma in children who had been exposed to asbestos, the sales for this drug went through the roof, didn't it?"

"Yes, the sales of Canbintrine for children have been extremely robust in the past year."

"In fact, prior to this latest scare, the sales of Canbintrine for children were less than a thousand units a year. This drug really didn't have a market, since mesothelioma was so unusual in children. And since Canbintrine for children is marketed for children, it was very difficult to actually sell a lot of these units prior to this latest scare, isn't that right?"

"I wouldn't say that."

"Oh, Canbintrine for children sold modestly well. Nothing compared to Canbintrine for adults, which has sold millions since the drug has come out. But Canbintrine for children was only selling about a thousand units a year, mainly to wealthy paranoid parents afraid that their children were nominally exposed to asbestos through their crayons and talcum powder. But at $1,000 a month for this drug, it just wasn't flying off the shelves, was it?"

William chose this moment to pivot and deflect. "I know what you're getting at, and that is that this drug is overpriced. You liberals are always the same. You don't take into account that the research and development costs for these drugs is astronomical and we can't sell the drugs for hardly anything overseas. So yes, we do try to get a robust price from our American market. It's called capitalism."

I sighed. I wasn't prepared for his filibustering, but, at the same time, I knew it was making him look awful. "The point of the matter is, insurance companies were not paying for this drug because parents were hard-pressed to show it was necessary for their child to take. Everybody knows that asbestos has been outlawed for the most part in the United States for quite a few years, so parents would have a hard time trying show the insurance companies that their child had been exposed to asbestos in such a quantity that this drug would be needed. So very few parents could afford this drug. Now, however, insurance companies are covering it if the parent can show their child had been exposed to the Spiritus dry inhaler. Isn't that right?"

He opened his mouth and shut it. "Yes, that's correct."

"Approximately 10,000 of the Spiritus dry inhalers were sold in the past year and all 10,000 of those were contaminated with asbestos, weren't they?"

"Yes, that's right. It seems that every parent who had that inhaler that had it tested, showed it was contaminated with asbestos. I know that's your next question so I'm beating you to it."

"That certainly made Canbintrine easier to market, didn't it? The fact that insurance companies were covering Canbintrine for parents whose children are exposed to your inhaler meant the cost barrier was alleviated considerably."

"Yes, it is always easier when insurance companies agree to cover our pharmaceuticals."

"Let's assume for the sake of argument that it was only the 10,000 parents whose children were exposed to contaminated inhalers who were able to have the Canbintrine drug covered by their insurance companies. Let's just see. 10,000 parents whose insurance companies are paying $1000 a month for the Canbintrine. That's $10 million a month that Tiberius is suddenly making on the Canbintrine and this drug has to be taken for five years. That's $600 million Tiberius can expect to make off this drug over a five-year period. But it's not just parents whose children were exposed to the Spiritus inhalers who are buying this drug. They're not covered by insurance if their child was not exposed to one of your inhalers, but many parents are still desperate enough to actually buy your drug and pay for it out-of-pocket."

"That's true."

"How many units of Canbintrine for children is Tiberius currently selling?" I asked.

"It has sold about 50,000 since the scare."

"50,000 units. 50,000 units of a drug that, before the scare, was only selling a thousand a year because of the cost. That's what, $50 million a month Tiberius has started taking in through the sales of Canbintrine for children? That means Tiberius will be making untold billions of dollars off this drug, all because your company caused a scare for parents all over the world that their child would die a slow and painful death from mesothelioma. Isn't that right?"

"I don't know what you're getting at."

Oh, come on. This guy was not that dense. He knew exactly what I was getting at. He could picture himself in an orange jumpsuit, living his life out in disgrace behind bars, because of what he did. I knew he was thinking this.

He had to have been thinking this.

"You don't know what I'm getting at. You own a shell company that owns 100% of the company making money hand over fist by manufacturing a drug necessitated by the intentional act that your company took in contaminating dry inhalers marketed to children with asbestos. Are you asking the court to believe that it's a coincidence that your company's dry inhalers caused a worldwide panic that children everywhere would be diagnosed with mesothelioma because of your inhalers, and that you just happened to be 100% owner of a company manufacturing a drug that addresses the problem that your other company, Columba, created? Is that what you're trying to say? That was all a coincidence? A very happy coincidence? Suddenly, you are personally pocketing millions of dollars a month off this drug. And wouldn't you know it, your company, Columba, is why you're able to pocket those millions of dollars off this drug. That was just happy kismet, wasn't it?"

He took a deep breath. "I know it looks bad. But, yes, it was all a coincidence."

"Again, I'm going to explain to the jury what happened. Isn't it true that, two years ago, right before you hired Andrew Garvey, you were frustrated with the slow sales of this drug, Canbintrine for children, that your company, the company your shell corporation owns 100% of, was manu-

The Trial

facturing. Isn't it true that at that time, you decided to take matters into your own hands and so you caused a panic that would mean people would stampede for this drug. Isn't that right?"

"That's not right."

"And then you knew that you were going to have to pin the contaminated inhalers on somebody, and you knew Andrew Garvey, being a suicidal man who lost his daughter through mesothelioma, would be the perfect person to manipulate. You knew he was a weak man, a depressed man, and you knew that if you told him that if he committed suicide, you would make his death mean something and that children would benefit from it and so would his beloved wife, that you could get him to go along with it. You knew you could get him to confess to contaminating the inhalers, and, most importantly, you knew that you could get those inhalers past him. After all, he was the final line of defense, the final inspector, and you knew you could get him to sign off on these inhalers."

"Why would he do that? If the inhalers were contaminated, why would he allow them through?"

"Because you told him, and he apparently believed you, that he was doing good for society in letting these inhalers go out into the world. You told him, and he believed you, that if children were being diagnosed with mesothelioma, a lot more research would be done on the disease. You convinced him and that's why he decided to let those contaminated inhalers through. Isn't that right?"

"That doesn't make any sense. Why would anybody want to sicken children, just because they want future children to not be sickened?"

"Because you convinced him that was the right thing. You contaminated the inhalers, you made sure his signature was visible on every one of them, and then you made plans to pin the entire blame on him as a lone wolf you could not foresee would do something like this. You took a weak, depressed man, you manipulated his brain, and he ended up covering for you, just like you wanted him to. He ended up covering up your evil. Just like you wanted. Isn't that true?"

He sat there, looking at me. He was not going to admit to it but he knew what he did. He knew exactly what he did. "No. I resent you saying these things to me because they're not true. They're not true and you have no proof they are true."

"Oh, but I do. I'm going to present these facts to the jury and the jury can connect the dots just as well as anybody else can. And the dots all point to my theory being correct – you did this. You contaminated the inhalers and then you reaped the windfall from the panic that ensued from your actions."

He sat there, silently. "I don't hear a question."

"Mr. Lanza, what is your net worth?"

Jack was immediately on his feet. "Objection, relevance."

"It goes to punitive damages, Your Honor," I said. "I believe that I was able to prove to this court what this man did, and, if the court knows he is already worth billions of dollars, yet he's out there sickening children with deadly cancer, just because he wants more, I would think the jury would not look too kindly on this matter. I would think that if the jury was going to award punitive damages, they would take that into account."

Judge Warner thought about my argument. I knew he was just as angry with this man as I was, but, the same time, this question really was not appropriate. But he had to also

The Trial

understand that Mr. Lanza was probably going to spend the rest of his days in prison for what he did, so he was not likely to appeal him if he made a borderline ruling that could tip the scales into untold millions of dollars in punitive damages for Frankie.

"I'll allow it. Please proceed."

"Okay, Mr. Lanza, what is your net worth?"

He looked over at the jury. "$6 billion."

"$6 billion. And that's not enough for you? Did you really feel the need to give children deadly cancer just so you could add to your already considerable net wealth?"

He didn't answer. In fact, in his silence, he was speaking volumes. He did it. He knew it. He did it for greed. At least one child had died and 19 other children were suffering, because of him. How he could live with himself and look in the mirror, I didn't know.

I never could understand that mindset. The mindset of people who had untold billions of dollars and still it was never enough. I didn't believe William Lanza was an aberration. In fact, I thought he was probably representative of many people of his ilk. Whatever. He was definitely a sociopath. A dangerous sociopath who needed to be locked away for the rest of his life. Which was probably going to happen.

Taking his silence as an admission of guilt, I simply decided to rest. "I have nothing further for this witness."

Judge Warner looked right at Jack. "Do you have any questions for this witness, counselor?"

Jack got to his feet and I knew he knew his work was cut out for him. To say the very least. And, for the next two hours, he did everything he could to try to rehabilitate William. He asked William about his charitable contributions, about the good he did through his company, how many lives he had saved through the innovations that Columba Pharmaceuticals had brought into the world. And, now that the cat was out of the bag, he asked about Tiberius Pharmaceuticals as well, and about the good Tiberius was doing in the world.

I looked over at the jury while Jack was talking. I knew. They knew.

Columba was toast.

———

AT THE END of the day, I brought on a few more witnesses, mainly some of the other doctors treating Frankie. I wanted to reinforce to the jury just how sick Frankie was, and might be for the rest of his life.

At 5 o'clock, or shortly thereafter, it was time to go. The jury was excused, the judge banged his gavel and informed everybody that they had to be back at 9 AM the next day, and I packed up my files into my box.

I looked up and Jack was approaching me. "You want to talk settlement? I mean, real settlement?"

I had to laugh. "No. I told you before, I don't want to settle. I want the whole world to know exactly what William did."

"Don't you see? The reporters were swarming in this courtroom today because William was scheduled to testify. That story will be out there. Trust me, that story will be out there. There's nothing that can stop that train from rolling along. At this point, I just want to make your client whole. And William has authorized me to offer a settlement of $50 million. That would more than compensate your client for the rest of her life. And here's the rub. The judge made some questionable rulings. One of the questionable rulings was when he allowed that email in – the email where Andrew was telling my client that he would commit suicide after the deposition with you. That was hearsay. It wasn't even borderline. I know you gamely told the judge that it was a state of mind exception, but you know you were using that email to prove my client had an agreement with Andrew for Andrew to kill himself."

"I don't see it that way. I wasn't trying to use it as proof of an agreement. There was nothing about an agreement in that email. It was simply a statement of fact."

"Nevertheless, it wasn't even borderline and you knew it. And bear in mind that the judge also allowed you to ask the irrelevant question about how much William was worth. I objected to that, because it wasn't relevant, no matter how much you said it was. The point of the matter is, no matter what happens here, no matter how much the jury gives you, and I'm sure you have figures in your head of hundreds of millions of dollars, we're going to appeal it and it's most likely going to be overturned. You're going to have to drag your client back into court in another few years, after the appeals court overturns the jury verdict and remands it to the trial court. In the meantime, while the verdict, whatever it is, is under appeal, your client will still be broke. She's still going to be living hand to mouth, dancing for money. But if you take my settlement offer, she'll have all the money she needs to take care of her son. All the money she needs and nobody will ever take it away from her. Her son is in remission now. That might not be the case in the future. What happens in the future if the cancer comes back and Frankie has to try another experimental procedure, one the insurance company won't cover? Imagine that your client has millions of dollars in the bank. She'll be able to pay for any kind of experimental treatment Frankie needs in the future. She'll be able to give him the best of the best."

I took a deep breath. Everything he was saying was true. While I really wanted to take this case in front of the jury and watch the jury turn the screws into this guy and see them come back with a verdict of $1 billion in punitive damages, I knew he was right. The judge had made some questionable rulings along the way. There was a good chance the case would be overturned on appeal, and, in the meantime, Lorinda and Frankie would be broke.

"I'll go to my client. I'll see what she has to say." I knew, however, that it was a foregone conclusion. A $50 million settlement offer was a win in any sense of the word. It was also a tacit admission of guilt from William Lanza. "But, no matter what, I think Lorinda will want a public apology."

"Of course. I will encourage him to make a public apology for making Frankie sick."

"I want him to admit what he did."

Jack sighed a huge sigh. "You know I can't do that. I can't possibly have him admit to that when there will be a criminal case against him. I'm sorry, but that's a bridge too far."

"Okay. Then I want for him to apologize to her in private. I want him to admit to her what he did. It will be part of a confidential settlement negotiation, so it'll be sealed and won't be able to be used for a future criminal case. At any rate, I want an apology. I want an apology for Frankie, for Lorinda, and for all the parents suffering out there. I want that apology to be a part of the settlement discussion I'm going to have with my client. Go to your client, tell him that's my condition and see what he says."

I held my breath, knowing I was bluffing. I hoped my new condition wouldn't completely tank the settlement.

The Trial

Because, when push came to shove, I really wanted that settlement offer. Jack was absolutely correct – I didn't want this to go to a jury.

Ten minutes later, Jack came back up to me. "Okay. William will apologize to your client, he will admit what he did, on the condition that the apology is part of the confidential settlement negotiation and will be sealed by the court. Your client has to sign an NDA about anything said behind closed doors. I want to cover all the bases to make sure this cannot be used against him in a criminal court in the future."

Wow, this guy really was trying to settle. He was desperate to settle. He must know, as well as I do, that his company's liability would be in the billions if he doesn't settle.

"Okay. I'll talk to my client. We can get the show on the road, the sooner the better. Perhaps we could meet up in one of the conference rooms here at the courthouse, get it on the record and get it done."

I went over to talk to Lorinda and told her what was going on.

"That sounds really good, but I thought you told me you didn't want to settle."

"I didn't want to settle before the trial, because I wanted the world to know what happened. But Jack made a good point – with all the reporters in the courthouse during this entire proceeding, the whole world will know about it anyhow."

Lorinda nodded. "I need to do this. I need to get money in the bank so I can take care of Frankie. I can give him anything he needs."

She would be a millionaire in a matter of hours but you would never know it from her demeanor.

"Are you happy about this?" I asked her.

"No. How can I possibly be happy about this? My kid is sick. I mean, he's okay now but he could get sick again anytime. So it's great that I'm getting millions of dollars, but I would much rather have him healthy. I would much rather have it to where I'm struggling, dancing for every dollar and taking care of a healthy kid, than to be an instant millionaire with a sick kid. But, my kid is sick, there's nothing that can be done about that, so it's definitely better to be a millionaire with a sick kid than a broke dancer with a sick kid."

THIRTY MINUTES LATER, we were meeting in a conference room in the courthouse.

After we sat down, I looked right at William. "Before we begin, I'd like to know if you have anything to say to my client?"

He cleared his throat and looked down at his hands, which were clasping one another. And then he looked right at Lorinda. "I'm very sorry for your child being sick because of my company. Your child is sick, because of me, directly. Everything your attorney said about me on the stand was true. I hired Andrew Garvey with the express purpose of having a man to manipulate to confess to the crime I did. I knew he was weak, suicidal. I knew he was mourning the death of his young daughter and that his wife had left him after his daughter died. I manipulated him by convincing him that what I was going to do, contaminate the inhalers with asbestos, would be for the good of society, and I told him that if he covered for me, for my company, and confessed to having done it, I would reward him by giving $1 million to sick kids with cancer and $1 million to his wife,

Barbara. I did all that. I did it because the company I was invested in had developed this groundbreaking drug and I was going to have to pull that drug from the market if the sales for it did not pick up. It was simply too expensive to manufacture and millions of dollars had gone into the research and development of it, but there was just no need for it. So I made kids sick so this drug could get off the ground."

Lorinda was staring at the spectacle that was William and I could see rage building inside of her. It was as if she didn't really believe this guy would do something like this, or anybody would do something like this, but, with his confession, she realized that he *would* do something like this and that he *did* do something like this.

"Here is what I was thinking," he said. "Not that it matters. But I was hoping that the Canbintrine would not only help children who had been exposed to asbestos to not develop mesothelioma, but that, if the drug was on the market for long enough, I might be able to get a patent for the drug to treat other diseases in children. The patent was for it to treat only mesothelioma, but drugs often become useful for other diseases other than what they were originally intended for. This was a promising drug and it would be a shame if I had to pull it from the market."

"I don't understand," I said to him. "Why did you develop a drug for which there is no market?"

"Here's the thing. The drug was developed to be marketed to children because everybody knows that mesothelioma does not develop for years and years after the initial asbestos exposure. Our market research indicated that would be a popular thing for parents, who were worried their kids were being exposed to asbestos in their environment. We believed that there was a strong market for the drug. However, as what sometimes happens, our market research was not predictive. We rolled it out, marketed it heavily, and found that most parents did not want to spend the thousand dollars a month to safeguard their children. It didn't help that most of the parents who had children exposed to asbestos, in old school buildings, old tenement apartments, and other places where asbestos is still found, were poor."

"So, you decided to scare everybody," I said. "You did your job. I admit that your plan was diabolical and genius. If it weren't for the fact that I had a source that not only pointed me in the right direction as far as the emails went, but also informed me that you and Tiberius were essentially one and the same, I probably would not have figured it out. It was a failure of imagination on my part to think that somebody like you would do something like that."

He simply nodded his head. "So I've come clean on everything. Let's get these papers signed."

And that's exactly what we did.

Chapter Twenty-One

THE DAY AFTER THE TRIAL, all hell broke loose for Columba Pharmaceuticals. All the newspapers were breathlessly reporting what was brought out in trial and the stock had dropped like a stone for the company. It also dropped for Tiberius, as everybody knew, because William's shell company owned 100% of Tiberius, it would also be on the hook for the plaintiffs to come. There was speculation that both companies would have to go bankrupt, and the pressure was so immense that Tiberius was forced to discount the price of the Canbintrine drug to $10 a month. So it turned out the drug wouldn't make the kind of money William had hoped.

The FBI had arrested William immediately after he left the courthouse. They were waiting for him at the courthouse steps, and he was forced to take a perp walk in front of the throngs of people who had gathered in front of the courthouse, because word about what he had done had spread, so, by the time he left the courthouse, there were thousands of people out on the streets with picket signs. He had to be arrested in front of all that and the crowd let up a cheer as he had his handcuffs slapped on him and he was loaded into the back of an FBI squad car.

As for Lorinda, she was doing great. "I'm back in school," she said. "Pursuing my dream of working with marine life. I'm not dancing anymore. Not that there's anything wrong with dancing, but, you know, I can't do that forever."

And Frankie continued to do very well. He was playing baseball, he was back in school, he was hanging out with his friends. Just like a regular kid.

I got the satisfaction that, through my efforts, Lorinda and Frankie would be okay.

At least for now.

Also by Rachel Sinclair

vinci-books.com/badfaith

A teen accused of killing her own mother. An attorney on the brink of self-destruction.

Harper Ross's last client walked free on a technicality, only to slaughter an innocent mother of two. Now she's drowning her guilt in bottom-shelf bourbon and teetering on the edge of self-destruction.

But when Heather Morrison, a teen accused of the brutal slaying of her mother, needs a defender, Harper reluctantly takes the case.

Turn the page for a free preview…

Bad Faith: Chapter One

HARPER

"THE BODY of Gina Caldwell was found and your client has been arrested. Do you have any comment?"

Flash bulbs popped in my eyes, blinding me. I felt bile travel from my stomach to my throat and swallowed hard. I had a headache that would have blinded me if those damned flashbulbs didn't first.

I didn't want to deal with this, even though I knew I would have to, eventually. Ever since my former client, John Robinson, had been arrested for killing his current girlfriend and dumping her body in a ravine, I knew this day was coming. My day of reckoning.

"Yes," I said, putting my hand over my eyes to try to shield them from any more insult from the popping flashbulbs. "My client, John Robinson, has a Sixth-Amendment right to counsel, same as anybody else in this country. I was simply fulfilling my constitutional duty in defending him."

My statement wasn't something I'd practiced in front of a mirror before leaving my house this morning. I didn't dream there would be reporters camped outside my door.

The Trial

After all, I lived in a quiet neighborhood in Kansas City called Brookside – I had restored one of those rambling turn-of-the-century homes the Brookside area was so famous for when I won my first big case and the offers and new cases came pouring in. It was always my dream to own a large older home and I achieved this. This home became my enclave, my space where I could decompress.

Now, it seemed, it was my prison. The place where the media camped out to get some kind of word from me about how I felt to, essentially, be an accessory to murder. At least, that was how the press framed it – I was the lower-than-scum who managed to free my client on a technicality even though I surely knew the guy was guilty. Blood was on my hands.

I didn't have time to think about what had happened to that poor girl, Gina, before the media besieged me. I was suddenly surrounded by all these people who wanted to talk to me about how I could get this guy off.

John Robinson was a Kansas City Chief's fullback who'd been charged with brutally murdering his business partner with a baseball bat. He owned a bar downtown and his partner was found in the back room, bludgeoned to death. I knew the dude was guilty – he told me as much. But he expressed remorse, breaking down in my office as he told me about how he came to fear for his life around this guy, and how the victim, a known drug user, charged at him late one night with a large kitchen knife.

The whole thing became "he said he said," of course, because the victim was the only person who could tell me what happened and he wasn't talking to me or anyone else. Still, it seemed like a pretty cut and dried self-defense case and I only needed to make the jury buy his story.

I also had to constantly quell my own misgivings about

my client's story, which didn't really add up. My client John was 6'6" and 250 lbs, while the victim, a slight Jewish man named Anthony Gold, was a foot shorter and one hundred pounds lighter. John insisted to me that Anthony had a drug problem, but I could find no evidence of this. When I did my investigation, I spoke with Anthony's closest relatives and friends, all of whom described a quiet, slightly nebbish man who loved animals and never lost his temper.

Not that any of this meant Anthony didn't charge John with a kitchen knife. But it certainly seemed like Anthony wasn't the type to do such a thing and my gut was telling me something was off.

I ignored my gut and went into the case full speed ahead, the media following the case every step of the way. It turned out John flunked a lie detector test, which pretty much sealed it for me – I was representing a guilty man. And I would give him the same treatment I gave everyone else – I would go balls to the wall and give him all I got.

What I actually ended up getting was a mistrial. The prosecutor introduced the polygraph evidence without warning, I immediately objected because the judge had previously ruled the polygraph evidence couldn't come in, and that was that. The jury was sent home, and the prosecutors, tired of the media glare, decided not to try him again. The judge ruled the jury was tainted by the surprise admission of the polygraph test and the fact that John flunked it, so there was no way they could make an unprejudiced decision.

And that was that.

Or so I thought.

I tried walking to my car, but the throng of reporters were surrounding me, essentially blockading me from my black Beemer SUV. They were all asking me for a comment, but, of course, I wouldn't give them anything juicy.

"No comment," I finally said. "Now please back up and let me into my car before I call the police."

I shoved a few reporters to the side, pushing one so hard she fell to the ground. I just rolled my eyes, not bothering to help her up. She was the enemy, or was part of the enemy squadron, and I couldn't care less about whether or not she tore her panty hose and skinned her knee on the pavement.

I finally put my car into drive and got the hell out of there.

WHEN I ARRIVED at my office, I could finally process the news that my client was in jail again for a brutal murder. Well, he was no longer my client, because my contract with him only lasted for the length of his murder trial, with the option that I could write the appeal if it came to that, which it didn't. But he was my client, and, because of me, he was free to do what he did to that poor Gina Caldwell.

I felt sick so I opened my purse and brought out some Tums. I drank a glass of orange juice and sat back in my chair.

This isn't your fault. It's not your fault. It's not your fault. If you didn't take this case, somebody else would've and he still would've been free.

I shook my head. It didn't really work that way. Alternative universes with alternative endings didn't really go in a linear line – if I didn't take the case, it was possible John would've never walked free, because perhaps, with his alternate attorney, the whole accidental polygraph courtroom admission wouldn't have occurred. Maybe a different attorney would've pled him out to 25 to life and Gina never would've met the guy. Who knew what would've happened if I didn't get involved?

As I sat looking out the window of my office at the expanse of the Country Club Plaza below, my mind kept going there - to my guilt in getting off this John, which enabled him to do it again. Deep down, I knew this day of reckoning would come. I always knew it, from the moment I was a baby lawyer and working at the Public Defender's Office. I always knew I'd do my job so well that I'd one day unleash a monster back on the streets and would end up with blood on my hands.

I'd been practicing for 10 years, and, thus far, it hadn't happened. Now it did, and I felt...haunted. Sickened. Like I couldn't get the picture of Gina - so young and beautiful and full of life – out of my head. Gina had two girls who were only 11 and would be without their mother for the rest of their lives. They would grow up knowing their mother died in the worst, cruelest way possible, outside of being burned alive. Gina worked at the animal shelter as a volunteer and had rescue animals at her home. She had grieving parents, devastated friends and a life ahead of her. A life cut short because I chose to give John the best defense I could give, even though I knew, deep in my heart, he was guilty as hell.

"Hey," Tammy, my law partner, said as she peeked her head through my door. "I saw you on the news this morning. And I saw what happened with John. Tough break, huh?"

I smiled, feeling that the words "tough break" were the most hollow, meaningless and understated words I'd ever heard. "Yeah, tough break."

The Trial

I didn't invite her in, and, ordinarily, that wouldn't have been a big deal. She and I always practiced an open door policy so it went without saying that we could always come into one another's office and bounce ideas off each other or just give encouragement when one of us was down. We often celebrated together when we won a big case. Ironically, the last really big case we celebrated was my getting John off his murder charge. After hours, we blasted '80s new wave classics out of our stereos and she drank champagne while I stuck to my sparkling cider – I'd just gotten my one-year chip from my local AA and was determined not to blow it – and we ended up going downtown to a seedy bar and dancing the night away.

Now I felt like the only appropriate song for the situation was a dirge. A funeral dirge. That was how I felt – like somebody close to me died. And, in a way, something *did* die – my soul. My ethics. My sense of right and wrong. What the hell was I doing with my life?

While I didn't invite her in, she sat down anyhow. She was sitting in the swivel chair I reserved for my clients and rocked back and forth while she carefully watched me without saying a word.

"What?" I finally asked her. "You're looking at me like I've grown another head."

She grimaced and plopped both of her elbows on my mahogany desk. "You're not okay," she said, stating the brutally obvious. "Listen, you were-"

"Just doing my job," I finished for her. "Blah, blah, blah." I felt the rancor building up inside of me. The rage over what had happened and about my career path and life in general. "No, Tammy, I wasn't doing my job. Not at all. If I did my job, I would've pled that bastard when he flunked the polygraph. I would've listened to my gut that was screaming at me to make sure that guy didn't walk out the courtroom door a free man. Or I would've-"

Out of nowhere, I started sobbing uncontrollably. Tammy came behind me and put her arms around me and I clung to her like I was a small child clinging to her mother.

"Shhh," she said. "If it wasn't you who walked him, somebody else clearly would have. He had all the money to get the best hired gun in the world. He would've gotten somebody who would've walked him just like you did. Don't blame yourself."

I shook my head rapidly. I suddenly felt I couldn't breathe. I felt like I was under water and my lungs were filling up with fluid.

"No," I finally said between sobs. "That's not true. You know that's not true. He was guilty as sin and maybe he would've hired a lawyer who would've done the right thing and pled him out. Or maybe that whole polygraph debacle wouldn't have happened with another lawyer and the case would've went to a jury, who might've fried him."

Tammy sighed as she let go of me and sat back down on the chair across from my desk. "What's this? I've never known you to have a dark night of the soul. Ever."

I looked at her. What she just said to me was *not* a compliment. Like I had no conscience. I knew there were attorneys who apparently didn't have a conscience, and, for them, winning was the only thing. They would take the news that John did it again in stride, figuring they weren't to blame. Only John was. That kind of thinking drove me crazy – as if, in a situation like this, there was only one person to blame. That wasn't true. It was never true. Yes, John was to blame, because he apparently had a problem with his temper, to say the very least. But I, too, was to

The Trial

blame for what happened. I was. There was just no getting around it.

"Dark night of the soul." I looked out the window and realized it was starting to get dark. I'd decided to come to work late after I found out the news and it was December, so the darkness started to fall at 4 PM. In about an hour the entire Country Club Plaza would be lit up which ordinarily would've cheered me up. Ordinarily. Tonight, though, nothing could cheer me up.

I sighed. "I guess I should go to the funeral," I said.

Tammy raised an eyebrow. "Are you sure that's a good idea?"

"No. But I need to do it anyhow." I dreaded doing that, of course. I would be faced with the consequences of what I did. Of what I set loose. John was back in jail, and, no doubt, would be calling me to represent him again. If he did, I'd hang up on his ass so fast...I'd represented repeat offenders before but they were low-level things. One guy getting a million DWIs, for instance. As long as these guys didn't kill people while drinking and driving, I pretty much took their case again and again and again. But in this case...no. Just no. I wouldn't touch that guy with a twenty-foot pole ever again.

Tammy put her hand on mine. "I'll be there for you," she said. "If you need me to go with you to the funeral."

I shook my head. "No. It's something I need to do myself. But thank you, though." I swallowed hard. "I wonder if the vultures are lying in wait to ambush me as I leave my office tonight. Maybe I should just stay here." I had a couch in my office as well as a chest of drawers in my closet that held pajamas, a change of underwear and a toothbrush. I also had two fresh suits hanging up. I spent the night in my office on occasion, whenever I was working a big case, so those things were necessary.

"Just stay here," Tammy said. "I'd stay here with you, but I have Buttercup at home," she said, referring to her 100 lb pit bull.

"No, that's okay. I need to be alone tonight, anyhow." I didn't really want to be alone, though. I wanted to be with Jack. Jack Daniels. I'd just received my one-year chip last week from AA and all I could think about was drowning myself. I was responsible for two little girls being orphaned and I simply couldn't handle it.

Tammy finally got out of her chair. "Well, I really should be getting out of here. Got an early depo in Harrisonville tomorrow," she said, referring to the bedroom community about 40 miles outside of Kansas City. "And gotta prepare for it." She put her hand on mine again. "You going to be okay?"

"Yeah," I lied. "I'll be fine."

Tammy left and I pulled out my couch and lay down. I fell asleep in my suit while I listened to the late-December rain pelt on my window.

Bad Faith: Chapter Two

A FEW DAYS LATER, Gina's funeral was held. I'd spent the last few days fending off the news vultures while trying to maintain a normal life. I'd canceled all my new client intakes and pawned off my laundry list of depositions and hearings to another lawyer in my building who was always good for a cover. Once I had everything covered, I retreated into my home and turned off my phone. I wouldn't talk to anyone, not even Tammy, who apparently tried calling me again and again – I didn't know for sure, because I refused to turn on my phone – so she ended up on my doorstep with some kind of baked goods in her hands.

I didn't come to the door, though, so even though she stood on the porch ringing my doorbell again and again, she ended up leaving. The baked goods were placed, with a bow, in front of my swing.

As I looked outside on the day of Gina's funeral, I saw the snow piled up on my front porch and the steps that led down to my car, which was parked in my driveway. I shook my head, cursing that I had to do the dusting-off-the-car ritual and doubly cursing I would have to spend my day at services for a dead girl that should've never been dead and probably would still be alive if not for me. The only good thing was the news channels decided to finally leave me alone as they seemed to get the message that I wouldn't talk to them. I wasn't talking to my closest friend, Tammy, I wasn't talking to my brothers and sisters or my mother and father, so I sure as hell wouldn't talk to them.

Wrapped in a heavy winter coat, under which I wore a black pantsuit with a black fedora hat, I made my way to my buried car and took my big broom and wooshed away the piled snow. I was running late, so I didn't have time to scrape the windshield with my hard plastic scraper. I had a small bucket of hot water ready to pour over the ice. I was always told not to do this, because it might result in a cracked windshield, but desperate times sometimes called for desperate measures, so I would chance it. It was an emergency way of getting that damned ice melted. Having to attend a funeral at 1, while just getting to your car at 12:30, would be just that kind of emergency in my book.

Five minutes later, I was crawling along the side streets of my neighborhood. The snow plow had not yet gotten to my enclave, so I drove gingerly and carefully through the neighborhood streets, until I hit the main drag, Wornall Road, which was thankfully plowed early that morning. I had to make it all the way over to Leawood, where the services would be held at The Church of the Nativity on 119th Street. As much as I didn't know what to expect, I knew one thing – I would have to face them. The daughters. The Mom and Dad. The cousins, aunts, uncles and best friends from college and beyond, all of whom would be staring accusing daggers into the back of my skull and probably right to my guilty face. I would have to face it and I would have to do it bravely.

I cleared my throat and looked at my unopened bottle of Jack Daniels I kept on the seat next to me. I did that because I wanted to show myself I was stronger than the drink. That I could be around it and not succumb. So far, I'd resisted the siren song, even though I was increasingly having weaker and weaker moments. I kept the Jack on the seat unless I had a passenger in my car, in which case I would relegate the bottle to my glove compartment. I was weird but I didn't want the whole world to know just how weird I really was.

AFTER THE SERVICE, I found the children. I'd watched them from my vantage point in the back of the room and saw how devastated they were. They were identical twin girls, Abby and Rina, age 11. They looked devastated.

I bent down to look them in the eye. "Hello," I said to one of the dark-eyed twins. They were both wearing tiny black dresses with even tinier black shoes and their hair was curly and notched up in pony-tails. "How are you?"

Neither twin said anything but looked at the woman holding each of their hands. "My name is Hannah," she said. "I'm the social worker assigned to their case."

"Hi," I said, extending my hand. She let go of one of the children's hands so she could shake mine. "My name is Harper Ross. I need to know what will happen with these children."

She cocked her head slightly. "I'm afraid I cannot divulge that to you," she said. "It's confidential."

I cleared my throat and got out my wallet, so I could

flash her my bar card. "I'm an attorney," I said in a low voice. "And I...

She crinkled up her brows. "An attorney? Why are you here? Are you a loved one or a friend of the deceased?"

Here we go. Of course everyone was suspicious of me. Nobody knew me from Eve, this was a private service and Gina had been splashed all over the news just about every night. The sharks were coming out and many more were kept at bay. This woman probably assumed I was there for the wrong reasons.

"No," I said. "I just want to make sure these girls have a guardian or somebody who will care for them."

"And if they don't?"

My heart sunk. That would be my worst nightmare, really, that Gina's girls would end up orphaned and in the system. They might be split apart as one family takes one and another family takes the other. They might remain in the system where they'd end up abused or neglected or shuffled around from one place to the next. They might grow up haunted - without a mother, without any family, and without each other. I did too many Family Court cases to ever think these girls would have a happy ending if they didn't have somebody solid to care for them.

All because of me.

"If they don't, I can take them," I blurted out. "I make a decent living and have my own rambling home in the middle of Brookside. Five bedrooms. I can even afford child care to watch them. I can-"

The woman nodded. "Here's my card," she said. "If you're an attorney, then you probably have access to their court files, even though they're sealed. If you're really interested, then start the process. In the meantime, we need to get over to Gina's house. We're meeting there for refreshments. You're welcome to come."

I wasn't listening to her at this point. All I could hear, if I read between the lines, was these two little girls had no place to go. They had court files and this woman was encouraging me to "start the process," which I assumed meant fostering the children in hopes of eventually adopting them. If there was a guardian in place, or, at the very least, a close relative who could take them, this woman wouldn't be saying these things to me.

That was one more thing on my plate – I was about to possibly be responsible for these two little girls growing up in a foster care system that didn't care a damn for them. Maybe they'd get lucky and be placed with some wonderful people.

Or maybe not.

They would roll the dice.

That was on me, too.

Grab your copy...
vinci-books.com/badfaith

About the Author

Rachel Sinclair was a criminal defense attorney for eleven years, so she doesn't scare easily. She graduated from the University of Missouri-Kansas City School of Law in 1998, and worked for the Public Defender's Office for several years before striking out on her own. She currently lives in San Diego, California, with her boyfriend, Joey, and her two fur babies, Annie and Toby. In her spare time, she likes to read, bicycle all over town, Boogie Board at the beach, and watch trashy television.